*THE AFFAIR AT
HONEY HILL*

novels by Berry Fleming:

The Conqueror's Stone
Visa to France
The Square Root of Valentine
Siesta
To the Market Place
Colonel Effingham's Raid
The Lightwood Tree
The Fortune Tellers
Carnival
The Winter Rider
Lucinderella
The Make Believers
The Inventory
The Affair at Honey Hill
Country Wedding
Once Their was a Fisherman
The Bookman's Tale
Who Dwelt by a Churchyard
Captain Bennett's Folly

BERRY FLEMING

The Affair At Honey Hill

A Novel

THE PERMANENT PRESS
Sag Harbor, NY 11963

Copyright © 1981 by Berry Fleming

All rights reserved, including the right to reproduce this book, or parts thereof, in any form, except for the inclusion of brief quotations in a review.

LIBRARY OF CONGRESS NUMBER: 89-62516
INTERNATIONAL STANDARD BOOK NUMBER: 0-932966-96-9

MANUFACTURED IN THE UNITED STATES OF AMERICA

THE PERMANENT PRESS
Noyac Road
Sag Harbor, NY 11963

THE AFFAIR AT HONEY HILL

ALMOST WINTER and the air like July; sunlight at a December slant, what came through the smoke, and the day hot as midsummer. Hotter, adding in the heat in the three gulps of brandy they had allowed him for his wound (his woundlet).

Waiting there now on the leaves and pine needles with the others, ten or fifteen of them it looked like, just waiting, as you did in a war (and in a peace too, God knows), waiting for he didn't know what, probably for a 'Fall in, you Rebs!' and boarding one of the boats, the 'Fall in!' bellowed extra loud for the ears of officers passing, waiting anyway to do what he was told. In the meantime, watching the boy in blue with the up-to-date Yankee rifle who might have been his grandson but for his color (not the Georgia-Carolina black of the prisoner with the corporal's stripes—head hanging as if he had been caught in a burglary—a Michigan-Ohio brown-black), watching the slow river through the trees (slow and fast as the tides changed, the Tulifinny) and the boats at anchor with the un-Southern names, the *Sonoma,* the *Winona,* the *Mingoe,* and others downstream with names he couldn't make out for the distance (and eyes not as young as they had been) and the pale smoke everywhere like fog, watching the yellow sweetgum leaves drift down with magic-lantern pictures for his memory of peacetime guns and bird dogs and ice on puddles in country roads.—Watching most of all the new memory (so new as hardly to have become a memory) of the moment at the spring, literally scarcely more than a minute: canteen smelling of cedar in the gush of cold water from the pipe—the Flowing Well they called it, the old man did and no doubt his Papa before him—musket against a gum tree to free his hands, not far, at his elbow in fact, eyes on the water, mind on the feel of it in his throat when he had drunk, the freshness, the slightly rotten smell of Low-Country artesian water when he had flung down his cap and shoved his dirty head under the spout, and——

'Put-up-your-hands!' (one word).

A grab for the musket, and a ball going through the arm of his gray jacket all in the same instant, the sound of the gun seeming to come later, the cluster of sounds, winging off into the pines and the smoke like a scattering covey of partridges, (the same instant as the flash-thought through his mind that nothing could please him more than being snatched out of all this turmoil as a prisoner, a piece—well-worn—"taken" and lifted off the squares of this deadly checkerboard). The black corporal then appearing out of the trees, prisoner himself under the gun of a marine from the ships, 'Loders' by then after a week's not knowing, and denying he had ever seen Daws before and Daws denying Loders, keeping it simple, seeming to understand between them that negatives might head off no end of questions before they were asked.—Which they seemed to do, letting them be tossed into the prisoner pool as just two fish hooked in the same bend of the creek. 'Do it yourself, dad?' with a wink from the sergeant-orderly in the hospital tent, binding his forearm with the good gauze bandage superior to anything the ladies rolled for the hospital cots in Augusta churches. And an impervious 'No sir' from himself, too content to be indignant.

And sitting there now in the smoke-fog, waiting, waiting, empty sleeve and bandage and the ache inside it all marking a change from what had been, what he had been,—out of it now, whatever 'they' did to him, wherever 'they' sent him, prison pen in Yankeeland or stifling brig in one of the big ships patrolling the cost (holding prisoner the ports themselves), possibly a candidate in a prisoner-swap, if his people would swap a whole Billy for a wounded Johnny. But out of it for a few weeks anyhow, which from what had happened in Savannah would be enough, the very thought of Savannah bringing in a double image, so that he hardly knew whether he was thinking of the great retreat of thousands or the small one of two.

'Didn't nobody tell you stay away from that spring, pap?' from a boy with a sun-blistered nose that had been following a plow no time ago.

'Canteen empty.'

'They watching that spring'

'I know that now———'

'Quiet down, you two!' (white words, black voice, and Loders rolling up his eyes in recognition of kinship with the tone—no look of any sort between him and Daws, continuing the pretense).

How Loders happened to be at the spring, the Flowing Well, of no concern to Daws intent on his own motives for going there, of which 'canteen empty' was hardly worth a mention: wanting to see the place again, or see again what it had been, what it was now placed into what it had been then, 'then' so many years ago he would have to count (and would hardly believe the count), wanting to see the months of 'then' that would be draping the water-sound like the gray moss, the young ghost that would materialize out of it, handing him the cheap hospital paper of the letter from the Lieutenant in Texas, '. . . last week at Buena Vista . . . left leg, not too bad . . . above the ankle, the bullet running round in front and coming out the other side. Five pieces of lead worked their way out while

The Affair at Honey Hill

here in the hospital. . . . Maybe limp a little the doctors say. Home soon as they let me travel. . . . Kisses for you. Howdies for the servants . . .', handing it at arm's length as if indifferent, really out of respect for possible eyes in the woods— nothing indifferent about Julia, a yes-or-no lady.

And hot as July ten days ago (more or less, he had lost count), at picket beside one of the toy trestles over the black creeks. Hot from the sun, and from the fires that had scurried up the pines like red-orange monkeys from the lightwood torches they had thrown into the brush when the wind steadied after sunup (bright idea from the High Command in the rice shed at Ferebeeville), the wind coming strong from the land then and promising to send the flames into their lines like a cavalry charge and drive them out of their new gun emplacements, their try against the railroad—'them,' 'the others,' 'the Billies,' 'the bastards'—drive them back from the tracks shined white by the polishing trains from Charleston like two rubbed gun barrels aimed straight at the bridge and Savannah, back from the swamp trestles patrolled by old men with hair the color of their gray pants, the one he could speak for scratching inside a dirty uniform and wishing he were home—home more beautiful from here than in the midst of it.

Driving them back with Rebel Yells and yelps and whoops and random musket fire to

The Affair at Honey Hill

supplement the flames, amplify their panic in limbering up the guns and caissons and carts of reserve explosives in the pine smoke and clattering off down the white roads to the Tulifinny and the boats, the cadets and overaged following on (a scattering of fixed bayonets behind them for the halfhearted—or more levelheaded), running and hopping over embers pink and gold and red like the paving in the Good Book's hell, until shoes seemed ready to flame up, thin-soled from all the miles they had shuffled, if not on these feet on others (probably dead). Belly-down, all of them, in an unburned woods when a company of bluejackets from the fleet made a stand, maybe blocked on the roads funneling to the Landing, Boyd's Landing, a rabbit bounding from a hole in front of him, this way, that way, in a witless terror at the Judgment-Day confusion (who wasn't!) and on to a stump between the lines and sitting there, not an ear moving, not an eye, not a hair, not, it would seem, a heart, then gone in a puff of fur, ears, eyes, guts, the bluejackets melting away in the smoke and Mathis mumbling, 'If we got no better soldiers'n them we in a bad row for stumps.' —At first. For three or four hours.

Then like a militia captain fumbling his orders, a rescue party giving up the mission, the land wind quieted down, turned with the deliberate slowness of a country wagon on a nar-

The Affair at Honey Hill

row road and after a short rest started blowing up the coast instead of out to sea, a light wind then that left the heat hanging and the woodsmoke smell, the fires dying out as they ate into the bogs along the creeks and the river as though they were an old-man's short-lived courage meeting his long-lived common sense. A reborn quiet falling, and an order passed along that pulled them back as into a vacuum, sucked them out of it: Sibley leading in a farm boy from Ohio, sitting him down, giving him water, collecting a handful of crackers from two or three and watching him gobble them down, and saying to him, 'If we turn you loose will you fight us again?' and the boy saying, 'I sure God will!' and everybody laughing, until they stopped to beat out the flames in the uniform of a bareheaded cadet dead on the embers, then laughing again at a ramrod shot so deep into a tree trunk nobody could free it—'Somebody run out of bullets!', 'Bastard in a hurry!', and such things —(magic-lantern flash on his memory of the yellow-haired student in the Philadelphia life class telling of an opera in Germany and a sword in a tree no one could pull out), then on to the station and their Colonel Robb on a stretcher being pushed through the window of the hospital train like a loaf of bread into the oven.

Not the overwhelming stroke they hoped for, counted on, the first young flames popping in the dry sledge like strings of firecrackers, but even so, with the follow-up and the artillery at Grahamville and as good a volume of musket fire as could be expected from militia (the Captain said), even so a success of a sort in forcing them back to the landing place and the boats, the tracks out of range from there. Not into the boats. They weren't re-embarking, the word was, but throwing up works round the high ground of the Landing, maybe to make another stab tomorrow. Or maybe to cover a withdrawal in the night (you could hear anything), the boats there ready, *Harvest Moon, Pawnee, Pontiac* and the rest, as out-of-place in the swamps of the Tulifinny River as he was.

'Pap' and 'Pop' and 'Dad' to most of them, with their soft new cottonfield beards, and probably 'Grandpap' to the beardless cadets from Charleston, parade uniforms already spotted and torn, (at heart regarding him, he suspected, as more of an enemy than the Yanks, cutting short their talk if he passed near as if he were a spy —he and his, what? fifty-seven birthdays? no, fifty-eight). And literally out-of-place, having signed for service in Georgia only, (' "Georgia only"? Oh yes, sure, sign your name right here, can you write?'), the Enrolling Officer for the SILVER GRAYS neglecting to point out the 'except in an emergency' coiled in one of the paragraphs ready to strike, and of course not

The Affair at Honey Hill

even aware of the words about to come down out of Richmond: *The law which restricts reserve troops to service within their State is hereby suspended.*

Emergency no one would deny this was, then and now, calling for everything they had left, which wasn't much, every man, willing and unwilling. And half-willing from unwilling, such as himself when he saw where they were taking him—to Savannah then over the river to Carolina, saw the rice fields again (flooded this time) from the cars and the rice dams and canals and causeways, saw FEREBEEVILLE on a station shed, heard somebody say, 'Honey Hill' (or maybe heard himself), coming round to all of it again in a circle eighteen years in circumference, or not quite a circle, a spiral in its not quite joining up, thirty-nine birthdays then, far down the curve. A different breed of words for his ears, then and now: then such peaceful words as 'Hope you can read my hand, Mr. Daws,' showing a page of the vast *History of the House of God* ('House' sometimes seeming to Daws to mean, not the Church but the House at Honey Hill, with morning and evening prayers in the parlor for everyone, white, black and brown, and a wide variety of blessings for all meals— the lady occasionally tapping restless fingers on the tablecloth); and now, 'Load!' 'Aim!' 'Fire!' and all the rest.

And 'Hold the railroad!' now. Supply line to the garrison in Savannah, and the only one, the ones through Georgia being heated red-hot by jubilant strangers from Indiana and Illinois and wrapped round trees or jubilantly laid on piles of burning crossties to bend of their own weight. And the only railroad, though nobody seemed to dwell on it, for pulling the garrison out if worse came to worst. Which was just what it was coming to, as anyone could see and none but a few of the worriers (overaged, usually) took a pause to see; for the rest Next Week hadn't come into view yet, hazed over by Today as the sun was hazed over by the heat and the smoke until it was a white disk you could look straight at—a white dish on old Ferebee's table, or rather in old Ferebee's kitchen for the house servants, the dishes in the dining room bordered with wreaths of pale blue and deep blue, the window opposite to him and at her back, her face almost invisible except at night with the lamp on the table, and not much easier to see beyond the lamp than before the window, fixing in his mind from that day to this a tie between something difficult to grasp or understand or 'see' and the lady in the dining room at Honey Hill—that was hardly a hill, an easy rise of fifteen or twenty feet above the fields and wooded flatlands, house toward the back in the midst of pink chimneys with watchdog lightning rods (in

The Affair at Honey Hill

case of mere electric storms, not shot and shell), wide porch like a hatbrim, a morning end, an evening end ('evening' in the Georgia sense of afternoon), a jogglingboard at the ocean end like a scrapbook reminder of when the children were little.

And down the seaward slope by steps of split cypress logs pegged in the sand, the spring, the Flowing Well, spouting three or four inches above the pipe and splashing in a noisy self-contained mythic sort of plunge that he heard for the first time from the buggy, passing it as Loders drove him from the whitewashed sheds at Ferebeeville. The station two miles from the house (that seemed longer, night, the misty rain blowing in) and about the same from the trestle over his head, already announced that day, introduced, presented, by the conductor with his 'Ferebeeville?' (up) and 'Ferebeeville!' (down), pushing in the round-topped door by the stove, himself already lifting down his valise flaky from disuse in his father's day, as in his own, conscious of the brief drum-roll of the wheels over creek-water that hadn't changed in all the years from then to now, then in the ears of part-time clerk on leave from the Widow Bray—'BRAY'S: NEW & OLD BOOKS, (General Agent for Appleton's *New American Cyclopedia,* 16 vols.)' —and this time, how many days ago?, the ears of a soldier (for want of a better word). Two miles on to Ferebeeville and two angled off toward the coast and the Tulifinny to the Reverend Trezevant Ferebee, to Honey Hill, to the lady at the top of the porch steps, by command it seemed, gazing at nothing, over his head at nothing, solemn-eyed, no smile of greeting, and the old man beside her peering straight at him as if appraising him for admission through the Pearly Gates. But admitting him.

'Mr. Daws?' through the ten-inch beard, untrimmed. 'Come in, come in. Take his boxes, Loders, Gilbert, Rosanna' (his single dried-out valise). 'Welcome to Honey Hill. This is Mr. Daws from Georgia, Julia-honey. My daughter Mrs. Ferebee, Mr. Daws, my son's wife. Miss Olivia—my wife Miss Olivia—is a little under the weather this evening, sends her regrets for not being here to greet you,' all in a sort of projected pulpit voice. No word out of the lady, the 'daughter,' a chilly hand freed for a moment from her shawl, the hand with the wedding ring holding the shawl against the wind from the Sound, the misty rain slanting into the porch as if had into the buggy. 'Come in, come inside by the fire. Cold out here.'—Winter could be cold in the Low-Country, not always like today——

'Hot as July, ain't it!' from his overage brother-sentry for the twentieth time, squeezing into the shade of a 10 x 10 supporting the trestle as if the sun had been a cannon aimed at him—

The Affair at Honey Hill

'Sergeant' Sibley (unfaded triangles on faded sleeves where his stripes had been but still 'Sergeant' to the rank and file, as once Governor you're always 'Governor' or Senator, 'Senator'). 'Remember that hot night the batteau got hung on the chain?' 'I remember.' 'Cap'm sent me up to town with the prisoner?' 'I remember.'— He and Sibley, real sergeant then, with the GRAYS manning the big gun on the cliff below Augusta, ('A plateau on the Savannah River projecting out from a high adjacent bluff somewhat like West Point,' the Mayor had written Richmond with a patriotic exaggeration, asking leave to close the river at that place. And getting it). The Captain passing a chain across, or ordering it across through a megaphone from the dry plateau, rafts supporting it, the whole barrier bowed out on the orange current and gurgling like a millrace. Toward morning one night, cooler than the day but still steaming down among the trees as if simmering in a deep kettle, no sound but the bubbling water and owls and bullfrogs and swamp sounds and maybe a catfish breaking the surface and the river slapping the rafts, then a sort of jingle on the Carolina side that might have been a log moving the chain or an otter or nothing at all, and the whole swamp seeming to explode as some old jumpy sentry pulled his trigger: 'Somebody over there!'

'Ain't nobody over there!' 'You got itchy fingers!' 'You having bad dreams!' and so on. Two Southern-made Colt Navy Repeaters in the boat but only one man, in fieldhand clothes, wet and dirty. 'Just trying to make it to Savannah in time to say good-by to my poor dying mamma.' And nobody else to be found though they searched up and down on foot and in boats until the *Leesburg* came. Found a second paddle but the prisoner said he always carried a spare, fool if you didn't.

'Tie him up!'

So they tied his wrists and Sergeant **Sibley** took him on board the *Leesburg*. 'Cap'm said hand him over to the Provost Marshal in Augusta, and I said, "Yes sir. Come on, bud."— Hot ain't it,' moving from under the trestle as if to give the whistling train free passage over it.

And hot that other day (though that was really July) when he first set eyes on the Reverend Trezevant Ferebee. Recognized him— what he was—as easily as if the Doctor had pinned a label on his black lapel, walking heavily through the entrance of book-tables and display cases, slightly bent, gray-white beard, wide-brimmed blue-black hat, elastic-sided shoes, as obviously a delegate to the Presbyterian Convocation in the city as if he had explained, a stranger to **Bray**'s from his chin-in way of glancing about over half-glasses and chin-out looking through them at titles on shelves and if a stranger to BRAY's a stranger to the town, Daws moving off into a book canyon the way you didn't pull at your line on the first nibbling circles round the cork, but keeping an eye on him through the shelving and after a time edging nearer in case there might be a question from close by, saying nothing, just *there* like Officer Mike tumbling his nightstick with one eye on a Suspicious Character—who might break and run.

'*How to Walk With God,* by Thomas Gouch?'

Showing no surprise at Daws's rueful head-shake and going on to select other titles out of a pocket notebook and offer them to Daws over bottom lenses: 'Burkitt's *Help and Guide to Christian Families?*' A brief glance, then, '*The Great Importance of a Religious Life Considered?*' Waiting a second without hope and putting the notebook away with a forgiving, 'Not easy to find such titles in these troubled times but no harm in asking,' and a little talk of this and that, his journey in the cars up from Honey Hill Plantation in the Tidewater, studying the flat cabinets of Uchee arrowheads and spear points and knives, the trays of bird eggs and butterflies (that Professor Bray had turned to in his retirement as a coach might send in a new pitcher for the last inning), polishing his glasses and holding them up to the window with the reversed BRAY's on it—which needed polishing more—and leaving emptyhanded.

Then months later, maybe a year, (days dragging, weeks leaping, Daws putting in hours copying the Doré illustrations in the new *Don Quixote* the publisher had sent them by mistake —hoping to supplant in his mind the beautiful Miss Sarah-D Hasty who had already supplanted him in favor of the visiting Lieutenant at the Arsenal), an envelope postmarked 'Ferebeeville, S. C.' one day, Daws glancing away at the nearly empty iron beehive of wrapping string and wondering if there was still enough for parceling up a nice order the old man had been studying over all this time. And finding a page in an almost illegible hand that translated into his having made inquiries about Mr. Daws and found him highly spoken of as a College of New Jersey man and one conversant with books, and was now presuming to ask if Mr. Daws might find it in his interest to assume the task of coming to Honey Hill in the capacity of copyist for his manuscript of *A History of the House of God,* the first volume of some 800 holograph pages almost done, with a second to follow and possibly a third. The copyist would reside at Honey Hill as an intimate of the family while the work was being carried forward, and he was prepared to offer $100 for each volume copied

The Affair at Honey Hill

and transportation both ways in the cars—all of it rising up out of the years like the smoke clouds of disaster piling up over the towns and farms of middle Georgia, Atlanta discarded, smoldering like the stub of one of the General's castaway cigars (that Sibley had told him about, and was getting ready to tell him again). 'I never told you the rest of it.' 'I think you did.' 'You know what a jogglingboard is?' 'Certainly.'

'I led him across this jogglingboard gangplank to the *Leesburg* on a plowline like a calf, sat us down on some empty boxes by the rail. Said his name was Wicklow. Nothing to prove it, no papers, no uniform, no nothing. I said, "Maybe you're kin to Wicklow Distillery in Ohio?" (I didn't believe a word he was saying, prob'ly thought of 'Wicklow' because he had a liking for Wicklow's Irish Whisky). Said the Confederate pistols showed he couldn't be no Yankee spy. I said they didn't show no such thing, he might as well loosen his collar for a nice Confederate necktie, just teasing him, I didn't think they'd really hoist him, sitting there, beginning to get dark, paddlewheel plunging back there like churning day on the farm. After thinking a spell he said, Well, he'd tell me the truth, if I'd loosen his hands so he could remember better. I said to hell with that, don't try any monkeyshines or I'd plug him, and he said just so he could wash a little over the side he was dirty as a rat. I said maybe he *was* a rat and belonged to be dirty, and he said if he told me the truth would I put in a good word for him with the Provost? I said I might do that if he behaved himself. He said I wouldn't believe the truth, he wouldn't tell me if he thought I'd believe it. I kind of liked the boy, about the age of my Douglas up there in Virginia God knows where.—I've told a dozen people what he told me, nobody puts any stock in it, everybody's got his own war.'

'You told me too.'

'Did I?—Wicklow, or whatever his name was, said he was detailed to the General as Orderly last year, coming east through Tennessee to help Rosecrans in Chattanooga, on hand at the end of every day's march with the General's saddlebags holding a change of underclothes, his maps, a flask of whisky and a bunch of cigars. "Saw me with one of the cigars one night and called the sergeant: 'Give this man an hour's ride on the sawbuck and get me another orderly.' No question who was running Uncle Billy's army. Back to my regiment with a red-hot asshole when they let me down, glad he didn't say hang him, they'd a done it."

'But he was still Orderly the evening this man Pike came loping down the road, Corporal Pike. A rangy mountaineer sort of man, flat in the belly from going up, long in the leg from coming down (or other way round). Knew horses but liked mules better. The General was sitting in a rockingchair on the porch of a farmhouse near the Mississippi line smoking one of those cigars and thinking, flask on the floor, cap hinged back, silver cap. He was by himself, wanted to be when he was thinking, and he was thinking about Atlanta, not Chattanooga right up ahead but Atlanta way on beyond that, thinking about if he went on and got in Atlanta how would he get out? Some mean mountains behind him then, some mean Rebs. Everybody up in Washington would say he'd put himself in a trap and couldn't get loose, poor General. And he would fox everybody by just walking out the back door while the Rebs watched the front, nobody at the back door but women and children; he knew the country, had hunted deer all over it with delightful hosts: succeed and be a great general, fail and be set down a fool,— way ahead of himself, where he liked to be. Used to say, "Mind you don't upset that bottle, Wicklow, it's full of ideas!"

'Well, the guard stopped Pike on the road. "What does he want?" "Says he wants to talk to General Sherman, sir." "Let him through. What do you want, Corporal?"—Said he had a message from General Crook at Huntsville. He had paddled most of the distance, a good hundred miles, down the Tennessee, over Muscle Shoals, fired at all the way by guerrillas, found our people at Tuscumbia and got a horse. Crazy sort of fellow, full of talk, said he got hit once on the sole of his shoe asleep in the boat, "Nothing to it." The General seemed to take to him, sat him down on the porch steps (other side from the bottle), asked him a lot of questions. Married? No sir. Children? Not that I know of, no sir. Got him a horse next day, had him ride along with the staff talking to him now and then. What did he do before the war? What did he want to do when it was over, it was going to be over pretty soon? Pike said he didn't want it to get over with too quick, wanted a chance to do something bold that would make him a hero. Which amused the General and he told a Major over his shoulder, "Says he wants to be a hero," and it amused the Major and on back through the rest of the staff the way generals' amusement necessarily does.

'That night he sent me for Pike, sat him down (in a chair this time), handed him a cigar, said, "All right, you want to be a hero, maybe I can help you. Next year about the end of November I'll be in the neighborhood of Savannah, Georgia. I need somebody to burn the railroad bridge just above the city——"

' "I'll do it."

' "Hold on now. I want him to paddle up the Tennessee as far as he can go, get over the mountains to the Savannah River, ain't very far, float down the river to Savannah. He'll have to lie low and keep his ears open. When he hears the Navy is making a demonstration at the railroad near a place called Honey Hill that means they've had a signal from me, know I'm moving in. That's when he burns the bridge—"

' "I'll do it."

' "Think it over. Tell me tomorrow. Ten to one you'll be caught and they'll hang you."

' "I understand."

' "Take somebody with you, ought to be two if one of you gets hung, give him a cigar for his trouble," handing Pike a second one.—Pike says, telling me about it, "You want to be a hero, Wicklow?" and I said, "Not that kind of hero I sure damn don't. But he talked me into it, a fast talker. They hung him on a buckeye tree in North Georgia."

' "You expect me to believe all this, Wicklow?" I said when he stopped. He didn't answer and I said, "What kind of fool do you take me for?" I was cutting him a chew off my plug of *Brown's Mule,* I sort of liked the boy. I shoved it at him along the top of the box and by God the son of a bitch was already over the side and gone. Taking my sergeant's pay with him. We searched for an hour, couldn't stay any longer, night coming on. Paddlewheel might have hit him, hope so, doubt it. I've told the Lieutenant, told the Captain. Cap'm says, "We've got men on the bridge, Private Sibley, what's the matter with you!" They think I'm just bucking to get my rank back. We ought to have people all up and down the bank. Day and night. This Pike's slippery's an eel.'

'Wicklow, you mean.'

'Pike. I think that man was Pike.'

'Couldn't be Pike, Sibley. Said he was the General's orderly.'

'Wouldn't believe him on a wagonload of Bibles,' and on in talk about the General this, the General that, all of it fading out for Daws before the pictures in his mind of the General as visiting Lieutenant: young Daws, young Edwin Daws, (or young as seen from this trestle in the Tulifinny swamp), just outside the entrance to the drill hall at the Augusta Arsenal. Waiting among the little ornamental pyramids of varnished cannonballs with others of the town's bachelors in inglorious black contrast to the braid and brass and dash of their military hosts,—himself there ready to leap to fitting the straw mudguard to the rear tire of Mrs. Hasty's carriage and offer his arm to her and her wide-mouthed beautiful daughter he was planning on asking to marry him, the Commandant and his lady just inside as if to silhouette themselves against the Viennese rhythms of his 2nd Artillery Band, three civilian violins from town adapting it to the ballroom to about the extent of a dancer hoping to waltz in marching shoes, the Commander having ordered up an Easter gala for impressing the visiting West Point Lieutenant (and returning the year's social courtesies offered him and his lady by local mothers with marriageable daughters).

'Mrs. Hasty!' from the Commandant. 'So pleased! My dear, Mrs. Hasty. And Miss Sarah-D! Do come in. Allow me, Ladies, to present our visitor at the Post, Lieutenant Sherman.' Pausing for the Lieutenant's rather too newly-creased click of the heels and School-of-the-Soldier bow from the waist, 'The Lieutenant has just escaped from the horrors of Charleston and Savannah drawing rooms, where he tells me casualties among the ladies were running high.'

'Please, sir!'

A bluff grunt and handshake for Daws at Miss Sara-D's, 'My friend Mr. Daws, Lieutenant,' followed forthwith by guiding her firmly to one side and entering 'WTS' on more lines of her card than was called for, she protesting, or pretending to, and moving away with Daws at last—or some of her with him, unusually subdued through the evening except as one of the WTS lines was about to flower and then produced the sumptuous un-Southern click at the cuffless ends of the red stripes.

Weeks—months?—of excuses more and more pointed when he called: 'Invited to Guard Mount.' 'Invited to Dress Parade.' 'Invited to Retreat.' Her poor ears rang after the sunset gun and lowering of the Flag. 'Never letting it touch the ground!'

'Yes, I've heard of that.' Trying to recover from what felt like disembowelment, a surgical removal of his self-esteem, a lowering of what he thought of himself to fit the absence of her thoughts of him; the book dust of BRAY's dry stacks seemed to add an appropriate suffocation of its own. The letter telling him the Reverend Trezevant Ferebee needed a copyist for his *History of the House of God* seemed to him an evidence of God's mercy forwarded on from Honey Hill. Changing him—and changing Miss Sarah-D into a child, Mrs. V. Grady Tarrentine within a year, but a child after the lady at Honey Hill.

Sibley still talking about the General: 'I figure he wanted to be a hero because——'

Mathis breaking in with, 'Psst! The new C.O.!' and making a nerve flick in Daws's chest as 'Psst, the Teacher!' in the days of desks and pads and hickory sticks prominent in a corner, a line of horses in file along a narrow trail beyond the tracks, the man in front buttoned up tight ignoring the heat, short terra-cotta beard, ducking his hat for a branch here and there of

The Affair at Honey Hill

the plunging water-sound in his ears as if making a continuous line under what she said. And when he mentioned the copying, that it wasn't half done: 'He'll send it to you, I'll send it. I'll write you. There're things I haven't told you. This letter's nearly four weeks old, he may come any day. He's jealous of every man I bow to. . . .' And more, turning away to the steps in the sand in a way that said their relationship had ended—whatever it meant to her, much or little (his appraisal changeable as the wind).

Watching the horses until the woods absorbed them, telling himself he was hardly even a name to Ferebee, 'Daws,' if he had ever heard it, covered with the fog of years now, ('What's-his-name,' she quoted him once as saying); no picture of him left behind, (as if it would have betrayed him now through the time-mask on his forehead, or the masking beard begun six weeks ago because of winter coming and clipping easier than shaving); no visible memento beyond the desk drawers full of his handwriting, which the old man had probably never showed him. More than a name to Loders—if Loders it was on the horse—but Loders had been, what? fifteen? seventeen? and had probably given him only the glancing view designed for guests (possibly more than that toward the end, from a window, down a hall, as Rosanna talked or hinted), but even a studied view had passed behind the masking years since 'take his boxes, Loders,' and no handful of dollars to remember him by when he left, needing the dollars more than Loders did. The old man would have known him—wherever the old man was. And the lady, certainly the lady—wherever *she* was, both lost in the eruption of the war volcano.

And yet not lost to Ferebee? Perhaps he had some news of her, some information strong enough to make him ask for transfer, bring him home? A quick sense in Daws of being closer to finding her—that vanished as quickly in the picture of unkempt Militiaman Daws (Militiaman X) craning up his neck to ask his mounted Colonel as to the whereabouts of the Colonel's wife! (or ex-wife, or whatever she was). But leaving behind a sort of shadow of hope in the thought of 'Loders.' Loders might know what Ferebee knew, or some of it. Find Loders, introduce himself, ask casually if Loders had any news of Madam, of 'Young Miss,' knew where she was. But how contrive to have a word with Loders?

Knowing quite well where she was at the time of his first letter, writing it as if looking back over his shoulder at the shore to see how far away he had swum, into another depth by then, another water-temperature. And finding himself farther away than he had thought when she answered, 'Don't write. You must not. Please!', the only signature a half-imagined trace of the afternoon perfume on the paper. And months further out into his life-current,— no figure on the shore, no movement, no good-by wave,—still needing to assure himself one doesn't usually die of love, a one-line note to her, 'Sailing Thursday Philadelphia *Gulf Stream,* Commander Powell. Must see you.' And through the brass slot in BRAY's door soon after, 'Addressee Unknown Return,' in what might have been the postmistress's hard pencil.

'What happened to the family, the people at Honey Hill?' the question for either one of the two women (either might have been the postmistress) in tan-and-white cowhide rockers on a Ferebeeville porch with climbing vines on the sunset end, the burnished rails across the street, he sitting on the steps, just an off-duty lonesome soldier during a stillness in the storm, between storms, an April day in January with more winter to come, a quiet to let the war-dust settle, let the mind become a tree and straighten up while the wind caught its breath.

'You know what he's talking about, Sister? I only been in town since Sister's boys joined and I come to make company. Two years, Sister?'

'Three years, four months and seventeen days tomorrow. I showed you Stovall's letter, Sister, didn't I? Where he says the sun was going down and the war was slacking off for the night and the band over in the woods was playing *Listen to the Mockingbird*——'

'The family at Honey Hill, whatever——'

'Said they found a song on a dead Yankee, in his pocket, *We're Marching on to Richmond.* Something about, *With weapons bright and hearts so light, We're marching on to Richmond. The roads are rough but smooth enough To take us safe to Richmond.*—Ha!'

'The Ferebee family, whatever——'

'The Reverend and his family, I know who you mean. Well, from what I hear they ran up on to hard times along with all the other gentry hereabout, fieldhands running off to freedom looking for a free supper with Uncle Abraham, nobody to set out the cotton, get it in, set out the rice, get it in. Sometimes looks to me the bigger you get the better mark you make for troubles to come mow you down. My Charlie, rest his soul, was a railroad man. Practically born on the Charleston & Savannah. Fieldhands? Shucks! Fieldhands nothing to him. If Mr. Abe had freed that engine out from under him he'd'a curled up on the tracks and died. Loved old *No. 7* better than his wife and children. I'd have his hot supper at the depot over yonder waiting to hand him when he pulled in for wood-n-water on the five-eighteen run, I knew just where he'd stop——'

The Affair at Honey Hill

yellow star-shaped leaves, the overage half-civilian pickets so newly in the war they simply stared as from a curbstone at the head of a parade—much as he had done on that indelible morning in the days of high hopes no time ago, of 'Parades, Fifes and Fine Feathers,' and the JASPER GREENS parading to the depot with their music, afraid of nothing but that the war might end before they got there.

Not much of a parade, this one; six horsemen. A Colonel, three officers, a courier and a black corporal with eyes pinned on the Colonel's neck (probably his servant, quite everyday), one of the officers pointing to something with what sounded like 'Colonel Ferebee' but of course couldn't have been, the sound of it tumbled by the engine whistle slicing through the humid pines and a moment later the 'parade' itself effaced by the cars drumming in a watery thunder on the trestle—in the same note as the other time, conductor in the round-topped door with his 'Ferebeeville?' (up) and 'Ferebeeville!' (down)—car after car now rolling between him and the six, windows full of overage-and-underage heads-arms-shoulders in uniforms and parts of uniforms, flatbed cars with chess wagons prophesying pontoon bridges like soothsayers, with black fieldpieces, limbers, caissons, forges, battery wagons shouldering a spare wheel like a knapsack, three open corncrib cars with sweating flanks of horses beyond the slats, then a caboose like the knot on a long whiplash, the engine already blowing for the station (as soon it would for the Savannah River and then Savannah), and the cortege had moved on into the trail up the bank of the creek, leaving him there by the black timbers and the black water with the underlining of brown sand and the smell of swamp and fish and woodsmoke—and the suspicion still in his mind he had heard 'Colonel Ferebee.'

Mathis the know-it-all answering his question before he could ask it: 'Colonel born and raised right over yonder.' 'Come from round here?' 'Knows every rattlesnake in these woods by his first name'—the man he had never seen? And (knowing his wife) knew the most about of any man alive after himself, and maybe including himself? It couldn't be Olivious. Some other Ferebee. No shortage of uncles and cousins—'cousins' springing open a bag of his keepsakes: 'It will make things simpler to introduce you as cousin, don't you think?' in the surrey on the way to a Christmas gathering at Rosedew (Thanksgiving maybe, soon after he came), murmured in his ear in acknowledgment of Gilbert and Rosanna on the front seat driving them. 'Yes, I suppose it would.'

'Will! You'll be Cousin—what? What's your name, Cousin?', and when he told her,

The Affair at Honey Hill

'Well, you may kiss me here in a cousinly way, Cousin Edwin,' touching a corner of her mouth with a finger in a white lace glove, laughing then and after he had promptly kissed her, 'Gracious me! I must say I had in mind a more distant cousin!' But gripping his hand for a moment. Then ignoring him all evening in favor of the young tutor from Bolen Hall, gaily trilling piano accompaniments for his performance on the flute, and not at all amused on the way home at the rhymes Daws had woefully put together, something like,

> *From Bolen arrived a cute tutor,*
> *Who was also adept as a fluter.*
> *The ladies would swoon*
> *As he fluteled the moon,*
> *Tootled cuter and cuter and cuter.*

'Agh!—Some cousins are as jealous as husbands!'

And beginning to accept that 'the Colonel' might be her husband (her once-upon-a-time husband). Not here just by chance. Likely enough he had applied for transfer, serving elsewhere and word reaching him of a battle forming in practically his front yard. Or the transfer might have originated high up with a need for officers familiar with the country, the tangle of roads and trails, the dikes and rice fields and canals. Whoever was responsible, his being there was coming to seem as much to be expected as the whistle, far off, of the second train following along as if linked to the first—and linked to the day of 'Ferebeeville? Ferebeeville!' and the old man and his 'daughter' under the high white ceilings, and the old half-blind Miss Olivia ('Old Miss' to the kitchen) moving about the great square rooms behind her stretched-out hands, and Julia's afternoon perfume on the stairs as if she were descending with flowers, ('Madagascar jasmine,' when he asked; 'a friend brought it to me from London'). Letters now and then out of Niger's leather mail-pouch, to all the family no matter whose name on the envelope, usually hers, 'Lt. O. T. Ferebee' in a corner and an address, one place or another in Mexico and then a military hospital in Texas, handing him this one (it had just come) through a patch of sun that made the white paper flash like a misfire, there below the house, by the spring, standing well apart, she in white for the warm day, April moving into May, the letter written in March: '. . . Home soon as they let me travel. . . .'

Then from close beside him a disconnected rush of words saying one thing in different ways, 'You've got to leave—tomorrow, no, today—illness, somebody ill in your family—anything, say anything,' touching him for a second,

'Didn't the old man have a daughter, Miss Julia?'

'He'd lift up his goggles, Sister, reaching down for the bucket handle, bugeyes, dirty face looked just like a barn owl. "Got me something good in there, Mamma?" Daughter-in-law, yes sir, the Captain's wife. May have gone to Columbia with the Reverend, a son there, doctor I believe, the oldest Boyd———'

'The "Captain," was he the one married the lady from Savannah?' anything to keep her on the subject.

'If you want to call her that. Lady from Savannah. Hear that, Sister?'

'Don't understand, ma'am.'

'Lady is as lady does, Mister Soldier.'

'You knew her?'

'Charlie knew her. By sight. Charlie's conductor, old Mr. Clydesdale, often passed the time of day with her if she was in the cars (to hear him tell it). Not sitting down, you know, not Mr. Clydesdale, just one elbow propped on the back of the seat ahead where he could look at her, I can see him now, fiddling with his white tie. Something about her.—Men are such plumb fools, Sister!'

'I wish these fool Yanks'd go on home and string their onions———'

'Even my Charlie'd watch her from the cab if she was on the platform coming or going,

33

sometimes Charleston, usually Savannah. "To spend a few days with Mother," says she. I've seen her. Hair in the middle, bonnet on the back, ribbons in a bow under the chin—oh my!'

'Didn't her husband have a law office in Savannah?'

' "Mother" up and died one day (soon after Miss Olivia passed, Sister) but that didn't stop her going to Savannah. Her husband the Captain, I believe he did. Charlie used to say the Captain liked the army better than the office, better than home. Off to Virginia the first gun fired——'

'I'd like to find her. Her friends in Augusta worry about her down here in the middle of all this, told me to find her, get her out,' (not just the way it was: he told himself to find her—and didn't actually tell himself any more than you told yourself to find something valuable to you in a burning house and get it out).

'She ain't "in the middle of all this," nobody at the house, everything boarded up tight. Nigger family lives nearby, farms a little, keeps an eye on things. Gilbert. He might know something. Comes to town now and then, or used to, haven't seen him lately, last time had a load of window weights from the house for sale to make bullets——'

All of it smothered under the deep clatter of the drummerboy at a corner of the depot as

The Affair at Honey Hill

though popped out of a cuckoo clock, turning this way and that, up the street and down, uniforms swarming into Railroad Avenue like bees out of a gum tree, a bugler appearing beside him now and firing the brassy bullets of *Assembly* at the north, east, south, west. A telegraphic dispatch from the General at Savannah: *Send me the Augusta battalion, the Jefferson battalion and such other troops as you can spare. The enemy has left his front, is advancing on this city. I do not know how long I can hold the railroad bridge.*

But the bridge still safe when the engine paused for a second on the shoulder as if to knock then rolled on over, car windows full of heads twitting picket after picket backed against the rusted girders four years short of paint, and by sundown they were on their slipshod march again, this time over the cobblestones of a street he suddenly saw was DRAYTON, the marker seeming to speak the word aloud—and in her voice: 'We were living in Drayton Street at the time of my marriage . . . Grandfather's beautiful old house . . . 143 . . . going downhill, repairs needed . . . no money to spare, Father gone, two daughters to marry off . . . Mother took in sewing' (never 'Mamma' or 'Papa') 'rented out the upper floors . . . usually to students, medical students . . .' (beside him once in a drowsing tone across a vast bed in a Charles-

ton hotel, the radiance in her face subsiding as she talked of other days, unfolded them as she seemed unfolded herself, stripped them bare with as little reserve as she had tossed away her clothes—a stocking had caught on the brass convolutions of the bed—he only half hearing her, half hearing '143,' his thoughts on the radiance itself, there in her face already at the moment of meeting him downstairs, eyes as bright and alive and in a way as multiple as candles in front of reflectors, and seeming to rise in intensity at each tread of the stairs until the unabashed moment of turning to him almost transformed into another person by the beauty of eagerness).
'. . . Uncle Jeff, Mother's uncle . . . president of some bank or other . . . always very fond of Sister and me, me and Sister perhaps, I think he was partial to me. He sent me to see Mr. Cohen after Father died—Mr. Cohen may have had a note coming due. M. M. COHEN. WATCHES, JEWELRY & FANCY GOODS. *Clocks and Watches Carefully Repaired*. Funny what you remember. . . .' She had been working there almost a year when 'a handsome gentleman' walked in with a fine old watch needing to be cleaned: 'The name, sir, please?' And writing down 'Mr. Olivious Ferebee' on the white identification ticket as he spelled it—the young doctor's bright new engagement ring on her steadying finger as Mr. Ferebee watched (30 per cent off,

courtesy of Mr. Cohen, who liked her). 'Where should we send it, sir?' Oh he would stop in, on Friday say? as he went to the train, no trouble, his office was nearby, *Brabham, Motlow & Ferebee* on Bay Street.—Her ring finger was bare when he came back though it was years, and several Julias, before he acknowledged he had noticed.

And 'Column Left' to a grassy square with a monument to Sergeant William Jasper, and by sundown he was digging what amounted to a shallow grave for Sibley and himself and buttoning their two shelterhalves together to make a merrimac, the city quiet as if hypnotized by the soft sound of cannon to the northeast and to the south, beaters at a hunt driving in the game.

And beyond the Square, on a corner (as if by somebody's plan that she should follow him) the church with the shallow steps that she had mounted without a backward look that day, no time ago, in the days of high hopes, of 'parades, fifes and fine feathers,' he in Savannah for Mrs. Bray to bid on a library coming up for auction in an hour, the band marching by—the big drum newly lettered JASPER GREENs in a black-and-green circle—carriages along the curb for the handkerchief-waving ladies and he in a space between victorias, watching and waiting to cross. A gaze against his face as palpable as sunlight, and turning then to see her in the carriage with two others as she quickly faced the street again and the belts and buckles and stripes and plumes and flags flowing by toward the railroad station as if on a downhill slope—and on to Macon and Pensacola (the picnic grounds), afraid the war would be all over before they got there, (in reality, on down the slope to Gettysburg and Chickamauga, and to Savannah and the chess wagons for the pontoon bridges and another of their diminishing store of retreats).

Watching her with a sideways stare, his face to the gaiters and cockades, wondering if she had come to see Olivious off to a second war ('Captain Ferebee'? today; 'Major Ferebee?'), a handkerchief balled up in one gloved fist with the stick of a toy Confederate flag. The years had been gentle with her (or so it seemed from where he stood), almost doubling in number— twenty-two then, she would be close to forty now—but it was as if all they had done was pronounce 'Julia' in a firmer voice, a little louder maybe, separating the syllables. As if she were now what she had been becoming, or noticeably closer to it. The music fainter now, sinking away toward the station in a sort of aural sundown, and nothing in the street but dusty mules and country wagons and a flock of barefoot children strutting to what was left of the band, dancing, tumbling, the coachman with his silk

The Affair at Honey Hill

hat canted backward to catch the ladies' next destination, Julia facing the roadway with the look of knowing she was looked at.

Following the carriage, but soon left behind, then seeing her on the steps of the church, mounting with eyes straight ahead, pushing the middle door and disappearing, and when he entered too (casting aside Mrs. Bray and library auctions), not to be found among the dim pews until his eyes adjusted and spotted her beyond a white column supporting the organ loft, she taking no notice of him or of whoever she might have thought it was entering on a burst of light from outside that ended like a dropped curtain, eyes on her hands or the toy flag in her lap, leaving him to imagine as he would which Julia it would be today of the two or three or four at Honey Hill—the distant Julia on the rainy porch, the Julia of you-may-kiss-me-here-in-a-cousinly-way, the Julia at the piano teasing the young flutist, the stony Julia at the Flowing Well sending him away. Or the one in the 'Don't-write-you-mustn't!' letter. Or even some new Julia. —Who might reveal some new Daws.

Into the pew in front of her, as if ushered there by his churchwarden uncertainties, sitting sideways as though on purpose to symbolize the mixing of eagerness and doubt, elbow sometimes on the back of the bench as he half turned, and hearing revelations from her that at first he refused to credit but that now and then crossed and fitted in with details he recalled too, increasing the credibility of suspect things he was hearing for the first time.—Not 'Captain Ferebee' had she come to wave good-by to. 'Olivious is in Virginia. Writing back bits of tourist news like a first-time sightseer in Paris. 'We can see the dome of the capitol, the fortifications round Alexandria, the Federal flag waving above them"—and such things. "They watched us from a balloon the other day." Not writing me, but Father Ferebee reads the letters aloud. . . .' The letters and the reading of them—again and again no doubt, by sunlight, by lamplight, through the polished half glasses—lifting him back to the other days, the other months, the old man pleased at the way the work was going, using almost identical words every night (except Saturday, Sunday tomorrow), identical gestures at the tall clock booming in the hall, "There goes eight o'clock, Mr. Daws. Very late.' And to the others, 'We have a whole day's work before us, Mr. Daws and I, and we must get our sleep.' And pleased with 'Mr. Daws,' once overhearing the old man's words to Julia and the young portrait painter over from Maybank (a commission in mind, doubtless, to do the young lady): '. . . a scholar too and excellent as a copyist now he is used to my hand. Already half through the first volume, six hun-

The Affair at Honey Hill

dred pages or so. Mr. Scribner has asked to see it. . . .' The painter saying something but unable to move his gray eyes very far from Julia, hardly to be recognized as the woman on the misty porch in November, as different as the garden path now alive with jonquils——

Not 'Captain Ferebee' with the marching JASPER GREENS but 'John,' laying the toy flag beside her on the cushion and lifting her eyes for the first time to look straight at him, at his eyes when she seemed to pause for some response from him and he turned his head to look at her: 'John? Boyd, you mean?'

'Boyd's in Columbia. A doctor. I mean John. John Trezevant Ferebee,' watching him as if waiting, and the truth coming to him slowly, (or what she expected him to accept as truth?). And yet was she really saying that? in effect, offering him his child for adoption? Or was he reading into it a confirmation of half-suspicions in his mind for years? Looking at her in the dim light and seeing the dimness of the summerhouse by the Flowing Well with squares of latticed sunlight crawling across the floor, and the whiteness in another dimness of the letter from Texas. And what she was saying now in a toneless voice coming through to him in the same double image or double sound of this day and the other days. His child? What of the brown-eyed tutor? What of the portrait painter? What of her trips 'to spend a few days with Mother'? —leaving him copying away at the old man's endless pages and hardly able to resist writing in a margin, Look to her, Moor, if thou hast eyes to see. She has deceived her husband and may thee.

No answers forming for him to his questions, no movement expressing anything, gazing at her over the back of the pew because he had been too unsure of what the years had done to her thoughts of him (or of what they had ever been indeed), and hearing of complications with the Lieutenant's wound that had delayed his dismissal from the hospital, the baby beginning to show but the old man too absorbed in his work to notice ('and just a man anyhow'), and Old Miss half blind, and little Boyd only six. The house servants noticing you might be sure but saying nothing—except no doubt among themselves but such things as everyday as sunup— until in a burst of emotion she had locked herself and Rosanna in her bedroom and, woman to woman, confided her worries (or some of them), Rosanna on the floor, arms on Julia's knees by the fireplace full of pinecones, listening but not much more concerned than at when a mare would foal. 'Births are not always as scheduled, Rosanna. Nine months, eight, ten months sometimes.'

'Do you know whose is the baby, ma'am?'

'Do you want me to slap your face!'

'Oh ma'am, no offence! Mattie says it's sometimes hard to tell, Mattie at the stable——'

'Never mind Mattie-at-the-stable! What would Mr. Lieutenant say if it wasn't born until August, what would he *think*, Rosanna?'

'I wouldn't worry, ma'am. Babies usually on time—more'n Mr. Charlie's engine.'

Then diving into it, 'I've made up my mind. I don't want to have this baby,' Rosanna moving her head as if at a familiar turn in an old story, 'Slink the baby, yes'm.'

'The old woman who lives in the swamp, what's her name? The medicine-woman?'

'Boomergail?'

'Do you think Boomergail could do anything? Give me something, some medicine?'

'Oh yes'm. Everybody goes to Boomergail. Snakebite, nail in the foot, Mr. Niger most cut his thumb off—'

'You've got to take me to Boomergail.'

Coastward off the ferry road, wading the ford at Bees Creek, off into a footpath along the soft bank, Rosanna ahead, horses in line on the narrow trail, down through webs of singing insects, nets of baleful wing-sounds above, below, ahead, behind, to the Tulifinny, across a tidal marsh to an island ('Cheeves Island—I don't forget the name') lying under a smell of old woodsmoke. And a wrinkled woman in a clearing on a bluff, skin black as the kettle she was stirring but with a narrow Indian nose that seemed at home in the spicy scent of smoke and bare tree-roots and the salt-scented mudflats somewhere toward the Sound. 'Cast the baby? Oh yes, Boomer can cast the baby.' But Missy would have to come back another day, the moon wasn't right today.

'Oh, I didn't mean today!' in a quick near-panic.

'Two days either side the full moon, Missy,' spitting a careless brown squirt of something at the base of the kettle and grinning at Julia with large even brown teeth. 'Then Missy tickles old Boomer's palm and Boomer sings her little magic song,

Full Missy push! Full moon pull!
Doodlebug baby, come out of your hole——'

'No! No, no! I only came for some medicine, you have medicine for everything, Rosanna says, just give me something I can take. I've tried quinine. I've tried castor oil. I'll try anything——'

'Must see, Missy, must see. Rosanna-girl, spread out the quilt for Missy.'

No! and No! that she might as well have swallowed, Rosanna springing into the hut like a retriever chasing a familiar stick, the woman taking Julia's upper arm in a grip of strong bone-fingers. 'No! I only want some medicine, something I can take. Please! Please!', words draining away—as if pleading with a man (the first man), and in a moment strong fingers like a man's pushing her knees apart and going into her, the brown teeth showing again and the eyes beginning to glaze (like a man's, if you watched him) and Rosanna beginning to moan, and herself rising on a narrow ridge of sensation that seemed to offer soft depths of oblivion on either side if she let go. And seeming to stumble on to a resolution behind her eyes and roughly pushing the woman away—prepared for a blaze of anger at being repulsed, and herself more than ready for angry flight except for the thought of the interminable wild woods to be fled into. And facing, unbelievably, a smiling 'Bring Missy back in eleven days, Rosanna-girl.'

And then, returning from beyond a floor-length curtain that might have been the jute bagging for a cotton bale, 'Give Missy one swallow three times a day,' shaking a green bottle against the light of the door until it foamed and the small animal-shape inside it dived up and down like a squid—flashing her mind to the small shape floating inside herself, and on to the girl Rosanna seeming now to be floating between Julia's world and the woman's, between the great house and the hut, so that whatever Julia did or said in days to come the woman would soon know.

Holding out a ball of money from the pocket in her crumpled skirt and accepting the bottle (repulsively warm from the woman's hand but seeming warm from the little dead creature in it), and dropping it behind her in the creek as they waded through; then, on the horses again and half a mile into the woods, 'I think I've lost it. I have!'

'Wait right here, Miss Julia, I'll find it.'

'Too late, too late. It's getting dark. We'll come and look tomorrow,' with not an instant's thought of ever being on this trail again.

On horseback morning, evening and oftentimes noon (she had heard it sometimes worked, or read it somewhere), alone at first until the old man, as if glancing up over his glasses for a minute from his sheets of scrawled, interlined, crossed-out paper, said, 'Take Gilbert with you, or Loders. Or Rosanna. Somebody. Don't go alone.' And taking Mattie from the stable; why, she couldn't say unless because of 'Mattie says it's sometimes hard to tell.'

Galloping away from her on the white sand roads, not for leaving her behind but as if for overtaking a fleeing rescuer, trotting back a way, then wheeling and off at a gallop again. Sometimes to the black river and the ferry to Haulover, sometimes to the tracks and the Ferebeeville station, hardly conscious of the woods and fields and new May buds along the road for

The Affair at Honey Hill

being so concerned with the bud inside her and a signal leading to deliverance, that didn't come. But another deliverance—a sort of self-made deliverance—coming to her one day fullformed. So that when Rosanna from behind, hairbrush suspended, leaned closer to say, 'Boomergail tomorrow, ma'am,' she said, 'Go to bed. I've changed my mind.'

A letter to Olivious, not making too much of it (second child, after all): would have told him before but hadn't wanted to lay another worry on his shoulders, such things being uncertain. And the date it might arrive of course uncertain too. She thought it would be (counting once again to nine on her fingers from the night in late October of his rough farewell—disappearing after a few seconds into his own particular frenzy as next morning he would more sedately disappear into the southwest), thought it would be July. 'But it may well be August, no telling. I myself was a ten-months baby, so Mother says' (lying), 'as I am sure I must have told you. Dr. Gillison seems quite satisfied, knows an excellent midwife, he says.'

And there one morning after a letter setting the probable day, but not the hour, or whether he would be coming from Charleston or Savannah, 'Yonder Mr. Lieutenant, ma'am!' from Mattie in a scream, and Olivious with a trimmed beard partly disguising the hospital pal-

The Affair at Honey Hill

lor limping through the sand, then seeing them and casting down his stick and knapsack to speed his progress and pulling her roughly to him as if halting a willful horse. And after a time standing back and studying her head-to-toe and smiling at her belt buckle (the square one in silver 'from a friend'—she had put it on without thinking, not knowing his train), 'Are you sure? He doesn't show at all, oh maybe just a little.'

'A fine baby,' to Daws now, feeling about her as if making ready to go, having told him all. 'And now a fine young man, young soldier,' fumbling her handkerchief, 'you would be proud. You saw him.' 'I saw him?' 'The drummerboy on the far side. He would go. No use to argue. They all love to play soldier.'

And he changing the subject to open a space to think in, hearing what she was telling him but not ready to accept it. 'How can I see you again? There's so much to say. Are you staying with your mother? Could I come there?'

'A fine ten-months baby. Maybe not to Dr. Gillison, and maybe not to my Rosanna and the kitchen, but nothing was ever said or hinted or "looked." Or not until later.—No, Mother died three years ago.

'With your sister then?'

'No.' And after a moment that might have meant much or little, 'No, I'm staying with a

The Affair at Honey Hill

friend. I have to go now.'

'Tomorrow? Perhaps I could see you tomorrow?'

'I'm going back this afternoon.'

'To Honey Hill,' saying it almost idly, a statement not a question, something to fill out her pause, to delay her, as a hand on her wrist, and being surprised at her quiet 'No' and a silence that seemed part of the No as if closing a book—and he thinking he knew this Julia from other days as he knew her 'Madagascar jasmine,' answering (or half answering) in a way that took him back to childhood and Easter-egg hunts and feeling, too late, if he had looked in one more hiding place he would have found the golden egg.

'Are you satisfied with "John"? You weren't there to vote.'

He brushed it off, a fill-in question that didn't reach to him as he seemed to wander dull-eared in a fog between a Julia too guarded to be dear and a Julia like a chain about his ankle he couldn't unlock (maybe chained by the very blanks she guarded).

And as if only now remembering (absurd as that was), 'He said to me soon after John was born, October or November, maybe it was spring, I don't recall. It was warm. Boyd was in bed, Old Miss, everybody. I was nursing the baby on the porch. Olivious was smoking a cigar.

It helped keep off the mosquitoes. When I gave the baby to Rosanna he sat without moving for a while, then he threw the cigar half-smoked over the banisters, threw it, didn't just toss it away. I can almost remember his words, and my words, but I won't bother with that,—I'm not play-acting' (the odd little aside breaking Daws's attention to remind him a No often included a Yes), 'and I'll leave you to imagine what I felt. What matters is what was said. He had been to Grahamville, talked to old Dr. Gillison in his office. "Would you say this was a ten-months baby, Doctor?" "The baby is normal in all respects, sir. Ten months? By no means unheard of, Lieutenant. I've read of a case in England, ten months and three weeks." "But this case." "No abnormalities of any kind. You have a fine son, Lieutenant." "But Doctor, *is* he my son?" And the doctor smiling from his rocker as if handing out a sugar pill that sometimes worked, "I'd guess Adam is the only father who hasn't asked that question." And Olivious, ignoring it, "I don't believe he is my son."—Or something very close to all that.

'Not looking at me but seeming to know I was trying to speak and pressing back my words with the flat of his hand. What should he do? (calmly in his lawyer's cold voice, squinting off into the treetops as if asking them). He considered he had three choices. Should he (one finger up) divorce his wife on a charge of adultery, turn her out with her bastard son—and set everybody talking? Create a scandal? A blot on the good name of Ferebee, his own, his father's, Boyd's? And assuredly bring the old man to an early grave. Or should he (two fingers up) say nothing to anyone, track down this man, this copyist, this whatever-his-name-is, call him to his door and shoot him dead? He could do it, he had killed more upright men in the mountains of Mexico. But a scandal too. Either way a scandal. Or should he (three fingers up) accept it?—moving his head to look at me for a second then returning to the trees. "The only end to conflict is somebody's surrender," says he. How many knew the truth for sure? Not the Doctor. Not this what's-his-name either. Nobody but herself. And maybe not herself, indeed. Turning my indignation into real anger (or you couldn't tell the difference). Telling me calmly, untouched by all my denials, my weeping, to sit still when I started to leave the porch. Suppose, he said, he sacrificed personal pride to save family pride and accepted it. Could he learn to live with such a grievance?—For the time being the baby (he never called him by name) and I would remain at Honey Hill. His law partners had written that his old desk was waiting for him; he would open the Savannah house and live there. Adding with his one-sided smile something about time was a poultice usually very effective with wounds.—Strange man. All men are strange when you marry them,' (the words, the silence, seeming woven into the skein of organ notes floating above his head as if from fingers performing for themselves, a skater alone doing figures on the ice).

Turning from her as if to see her life better in the dimness, the parts of her life she had left in shadows, and finding her gone without a sound (a shadow herself) when he turned back again, the outer door closing and himself with an immediate decision not to follow her, or try to, so full of his hour with her he seemed to hunger for a quiet lonesome silence in which to listen again—four words seeming to rise up repeatedly though they had been said only once, and then occupied hardly a second: 'To Honey Hill?' from him, and, 'No' from her. Ending it. Leaving him then and now as if peering through the mesh of a fence with PRIVATE on the wire and a far-off view of someone walking away at a composed stroll, someone who resembled her at first glance and at second didn't.

The organ notes drifting away over his head like birds flying off high and small, then empty sky, or silence, or absence, and he walking away from the void, from the Julias one and all, or meaning to, out into Duke Street. And then, as if followed by her and 'Grandfather's beautiful

The Affair at Honey Hill

old house,' on into Drayton, leaving one headful of thoughts of her and taking another headful with him to see the house where 'Mother took in sewing,' rented out the upper floors to students (one of whom might well have later bought an engagement ring from Mr. Cohen at 30 per cent off—and had it returned with probably a Julia-explanation), see the neighborhood that was such a part of her memory—and of his memory too, now, at one remove.

But no 'beautiful old house' at 143. No 143 at all. Broad sliding doors at 141-145 under a long sign painted on the brick in red and black, Livery & Hiring Stable, Est. 1809, (before her memory began); a small door at a corner leading to upstairs meeting rooms of the 'B.P.O.E.' He had forgotten the number? Or, incredibly, had she? Or, quite credibly, was she guarding the number (and even the street) for reasons of her own, beyond the barrier fence marked 'Private'?

Questions following him to the station, to the bench in the waiting room, deliberately to the very bench he had waited on between trains on his way to Ferebeeville and Honey Hill as copyist, changing then from the Central of Georgia to the Charleston & Savannah, waiting now for the C-of-Ga (and an inspirational lie about the auction that would satisfy Mrs. Bray), studying the railroad map in a timetable as if it might hold an answer, and seeing only a memory of the two lines using the same tracks for a few miles up the Georgia side of the river then parting in a Y, one going on straight into Georgia, the other swinging right over the frogs with a dancer's castanets and crossing the bridge and the rice fields to Silk Hope station (nothing but a plantation house back on a rise, a few white-mulberry trees still standing as if a prodigal silkworm might yet come home), and on into the pinewoods and black swamps and the drumming short trestles to 'Ferebeeville?' (up) and 'Ferebeeville!' (down) and Loders in the buggy and Julia on the porch of Honey Hill, and six months that had marked him like initials on a tree—eyes pulled upward from the railroad map and all it seemed to hold by two passengers hurrying past him to the trains, a well-dressed man with gray in a bushy moustache and Julia, on his arm as if he had just lifted her lightly to the platform off Daws's dream porch, the C-&-S conductor at the steps of his end car and touching his glossy visor in welcome, offering his hand to assist the lady on the box-step and being forestalled by the gentleman himself, the lady spurning both with a scoop of her hems and a light-footed ascent on her own—as though tossing Daws a farewell ambrotype of herself to remember her by.

And then a few days ago, 'Cheeves Island,'

The Affair at Honey Hill

from a boy with dark fuzz along his jawbone, VMI on each side of his standup collar and elaborate stripes on his upper sleeves. 'Yes sir, I can get to Cheeves Island.'

'You come from round here, Soldier, knowing Cheeves Island?'

About to say 'round here' was where he first saw the light of day, but trimming it to 'Yes sir.' And getting, 'Don't say Sir to me, I'm not an officer.'

'Yes sir, (pardon).'

Then suddenly all spit-and-polish, stiff as a new knapsack: 'You will make your way through the woods to Bees Creek and the Tulifinny River,' (the military You Will). 'You will relieve the picket on Cheeves Island and order him to report to me at once at these headquarters,' (these headquarters the cotton shed at Ferebeeville station, flakes of old whitewash still clinging under the eaves from the days of Parades, Fifes and Fine Feathers, two 3-inch fieldpieces in a scooped-out emplacement at the Savannah end). 'You will carry rations for two days. . . . You will occupy the post on the Bluff until relieved. . . . You will be constantly alert for any change or activity in the direction of the sound . . . ,' asking his name and writing it down, and the time (from a pre-graduation-present watch).

Squatting on the low bluff beyond what was

left of the hut, poking the fire and the two sweet potatoes browning in the embers for his breakfast, glad for the daylight even with the faked quality it had from the close-in fog, still seeming surrounded by the disjointed pieces of his fitful sleep (fitful sleeps), the incomprehensible gyrations of three dream witches calling themselves 'Boomer' and 'Rosie' and 'Julia,' all like as sisters and hailing each other as 'Sister' as they pranced, sang, snickered, laughed. Holding up his poker as if to shush them, hardly enough awake to know whether he was shushing them or meaning to shush the outside sound in the fog, a humming sound he wasn't really sure he heard. Then sure, and thinking it might be bees in the woods behind him, except for a throbbing it seemed to have which he was half ready to hear as the pounding feet of the Sisters, and looking up into the gray mist at the bullfrog shape of a sidewheeler forty yards away and coming straight at him like a charging elephant ghost.

Up to his feet with a screech, embers scattering, potatoes rolling in the sand, and himself grabbing the musket and haversack and plunging into the trees. But coming back and watching through the low fork of a liveoak as it passed—as they passed, scratching the names on the musket stock with his knife for the moment of facing the boy from VMI: *Pontiac,* side-

The Affair at Honey Hill

wheeler, bow gun. *Harvest Moon, Mingoe, Sonoma,* all screw ships. And the screw ship with a 9-inch pivot gun, *Wissahickon*—the name lifting him up and away like Chaucer's eagle, to a rooming house close by the Wissahickon River in Philadelphia and the year of his life he had spent in the studio of the man who proposed to teach 'the Art of drawing with the greatest Exactness.'

Hardly an instant by the Philadelphia river, then back to this one: not waiting to count the rest, the tugs and barges lined with caps and soldier-shapes, but crawling to the hut and past it and setting off up the trail at his old-man's version of a run, sprawling after a minute flatout on the sand and yellow leaves to catch his breath, chest heaving in a one-sided rhythm that reminded him of the clicking valves of a standing steam engine, but most of his mind on the *Wissahickon,* ship and river—and the man from Philadelphia in the door of BRAY's one morning, turned-up brown moustaches lightly waxed: would the bookstore permit one of his posters in their window? *S. Pondergreen, Limner, for a short time at the Globe Hotel where Gentlemen and Ladies may have their pictures drawn, likewise Landscapes of all sizes, Crests and Coats of Arms for Coaches and Chaises,* (all in Spencerian flourishes kin to the moustaches)——

And breath recaptured, on to another halt, halts moving in closer to one another as if about to combine into one final halt, at all of which Mr. Pondergreen and Philadelphia seemed to have arrived before him: *For young Gentlemen and Ladies inclinable to be taught the Art of Drawing he will open an Evening School in his rooms where every branch of that Art will be taught with the greatest Exactness.* Three even-evenings a week and hours besides at home and on a quickly concealable pad at the store: eyes, ears, noses, mouths, ('You're right or wrong by a sixteenth of an inch, young Gentlemen and Ladies'), all of it reviving in him a friendliness with chalk, crayons, pencils from nursery days stored away in a forgotten corner, (and sometimes from the same corner a faint brief view of the young portrait painter over from Maybank, or rather the glances at him from Julia that Daws peeped at). Often beside Mr. Pondergreen in the hired trap off to 'wait on patrons at their respective plantations in the country,' handy at stretching canvas, cleaning brushes, scraping palettes, gluing frame corners, and sometimes, 'If Madam has no objection,' making pencil sketches of his own. And finally handy at helping the little man gather up his paraphenalia and pushcart everything to the depot and the baggage car. 'Good-by, my boy. If you want to come up and help round the studio

The Affair at Honey Hill

I'll show you how to use a broom while you're learning to use a brush.'—And after a time following along by the steamer *Gulf Stream*, Commander Powell, into a year of new faces, new voices, new thinking, meeting old Mr. Nagle (in a wheelchair), seeing and listening and talking (into smiles at his pronounciation), and back at last, by train (trains) and standing a card of his own in the bookstore window: *Pictures drawn of Ladies and Gentlemen at $15 for a head. For the convenience of Patrons in the Country the Artist will be pleased to wait on them at their respective Plantations,* beside the card, as a sample of his work, a small composition in yellow sunlight and shadowy greens of a woman with her hand in a spring, a Flowing Well, unrecognizable because of the shadows and because he had forgotten; not forgotten, had never known——

And running on again, out of then into now, his next halting place revealing itself as a half-familiar stretch of white sand road that became in a moment the road Loders had driven him in the buggy—one way then the other, arriving, leaving, one Daws arriving, another leaving (and today's Daws still another—half-hearted soldier out of breath from running to what might be his own court-martial for leaving his post). Up to his feet and hurrying on, and gasping out to the first uniform he saw,

'Gunboats in the river!'

And having his disclosure emphatically confirmed by a shell from one of the guns—probably the 9-inch on the *Wissahickon*—screaming through the smoke and heat in what seemed to be the direction of the old house, the chimneys perhaps the only target the gunners could see over the trees, the railroad invisible (and out of range anyway), and needing to make a conquering gesture at something. And staggering into Ferebeeville at last, turning to see smoke, not covering the sky as it had been from the torches thrown in the brush but rising in a plume as if lifted off a shako of the JASPER GREENS, inflated a thousand times and planted here as though on a military map to mark an army's progress—many plumes to the north on the roads into the city and now a plume on the road out.—'Mutilated gunstock,' from Sergeant Spit-and-polish, writing it down.

'Nothing else to mark on, sir.'

'Wait outside.'

Waiting a while on the splintered floor of the cotton shed, invisible it seemed beyond the burst of activity inside, forgotten, then begging something to eat at a cook tent and eating it on a pile of rotting crossties watching the smoke-plume settling now behind the trees.

And on some later afternoon (the deck of days so shuffled in his mind they had no order),

The Affair at Honey Hill

gazing from the curve in the driveway where he had first seen her on the porch, nothing to be seen now but three chimneys, the brick courses at the tops stepping outward course by course and making funnel shapes against the sky like red-brown smokestacks of locomotives, the upper part of the fourth chimney torn away but leaving the fireplace of her bedroom and the vine-carved mantelpiece. Simmering piles of bent and twisted tin between the chimneys, a blackened corner of the weathervane Gilbert had installed on the ridgepole (the old man interrupting their work long enough to call him outside to watch the ceremony), the skewed angles of the lightning rod for warding off disaster—mere electric storms, not cannonballs—and down the slope on the seaward side the Flowing Well, still flowing, a watch still ticking in a dead soldier's pocket.

And the war still flowing too: black labor digging gun emplacements on the landward slope (Honey Hill readymade as a parapet but for the intervening chimneys), artillerymen on horses straining at gun carriages in the soft earth, caissons, foot soldiers shoving in hand carts of reserve ammunition, orders, commands, spoken, shouted, roared, and Georgia cannonballs smashing into one chimney after another until they —we—had a clear trajectory to the landing place and the boats, not toppling the chimneys like trees with seeds to maybe rise again but crumbling them straight down into dry low pyramids, the echo of the guns mingling with the rumble of cascading brick—and leaving him denying to himself he had heard his peacetime name, then hearing it again, 'Mr. Daws, sir?' at his shoulder, in a rising inflection more for attention-getting than question-asking, he trying to solve quickly the puzzle of 'mister' and 'sir' in the place usually held by 'Private Daws' or just 'you, Soldier,' and the puzzle of being addressed at all by a black man he couldn't remember, then began to remember though he couldn't say whether from a few days before, following the officers on the trail, or from years far back, then everything becoming clear with, 'Colonel's worried about Miss Julia.'

'Loders?'

'Asks do you know anything about Miss Julia? Where he can find Miss Julia? Is she all right?' Daws shaking his head, about to say more but Loders moving away, and Olivious, watching from under the trees, lifting reins and riding off toward the station: 'Worried about Miss Julia,' indifferent to 'What's-his-name' except as a possible means of finding her. Strange man. All men are strange when you marry them——

All of it blotted out by the drums in the black morning, the air with a daybreak smell, a

The Affair at Honey Hill

sharper edge, pine-smoke smell as yesterday but with a lacing of burnt gunpower blowing in on the sea wind that tied it to the spongy far-off cannon sounds from the only fort left between 'them' and the city, 'them' and their navy. Battercakes and sorghum, coffee that the young-enough-to-be-coarse said was horse piss, 'Fall in!' before the cones of musket-sheaves like a furrow of peacetime October corn, and a march without arms down the cobblestones to the wharf and black fieldhands loading the last of a pile of logs marked '20 Cords Dry Pine Wood' for fueling the sidewheeler *Let Her Be*. 'Where we going, Sergeant?' from somebody, somebody else he was glad to say.

'How long you been in the army don't know no better'n to ask where you going!'

Up the wide river that the spreading daylight colored as if with wash after wash of watercolor orange from the brush of S. Pondergreen, flat farmland on one side, flat river-colored marsh on the other, all level as rolled-out biscuit dough, everything horizontal but the matchstem smokestack of the *Let Her Be*, and after a time the marshes becoming rice fields and causeways and low dams you would hardly have seen but for the vertical posts of gates for the tides in and out. Sibley saying, 'Bridge still there,' pointing at a line of cars that must have just crossed, scudding toward the city under a blue-white

63

tassel of pine smoke. Then, 'If we up here to get Pike we gonna need more soldiers.'

'Two platoons!'

'Pike's sharp. D'I ever tell you . . .,' breaking off to join in the genial hello-waves fluttering up and down between the deck and the bridge girders like flocks of tame pigeons as the boat passed under. And before he could go on with it, the Sergeant whistling them up on the after deck out of the wind and announcing through the slushing of the paddles, 'All right, you GRAYS! We're coming in for a landing. You've come up here to get some pontoons for the General. You're going to wade right into these rice fields—ain't very deep—and round up every ricefield flat you can find, every one that can float. Bail 'em out, shove 'em round to a tidegate and out into the river——' 'For a pontoon bridge, Sergeant?' 'Ain't none of your business what he wants 'em for, Mister, your business is just get 'em for him like a Christmas present, like you're Santy Claus. Two men to every flat. Roll up your pants,' rolling up his own to his scaly knees, farm-bell *pings!* settling from the wheelhouse like leaves and the paddles suddenly still, brown water brushing affectionately along the hull.

Then, all of them out on the dock and in a line, 'Where's the sergeant?' from a man in a black bow tie, black hat and polished easy rid-

The Affair at Honey Hill

ingboots walking on to the landing from a horse standing on the causeway reins dangling as if tethered to the weeds. And the Sergeant, 'Here, sir! I've come for your flats, sir,' handing him a paper which he put in a pocket without looking at.

'I know. The General told me. All right, round them up,' with a gesture at the flooded fields. 'Ezra here will count,' nodding his head backward at a brown man with crinkled hair and thin lips. 'And both of you sign. I'll want a receipt to offer the gentlemen in Richmond and' (showing good teeth) 'get me some more pretty Confederate dollars to start my fires with.' Then turning back as he started off, 'Your men better keep their shoes on, takes a nigger to go in there barefoot and ain't any more niggers,' walking away past a set of rice scales in the floor with a final, 'Count 'em, Ezra.'

'Oh yes, sir.'

Along a dike with the others—followed for a few steps by the question in his mind of where he had seen this man before (or if he had)—then down over the rim of yellow-brown December weeds into a flooded field, in front of him a spray of frogs in long trajectories, insects up in a cloud, a marsh bird off like a hit baseball, the black head of a water moccasin trailing a neck scarf of pleated wake, and into the firm prickly mud of the bottom. Field after field, flat after flat, some as long as railroad cars; scoops in some of them and scooping out rainwater, frogs dead and alive, dead birds, dead lizards, a bleached skeleton of a snake—until he panted, 'Amen!' when a nearby soldier as overaged as himself said, 'I'd sooner be in a hole with Yankee lead looking for me.'

Pulled out at last by the Sergeant's whistle (the *Let Her Be* docking with a relief company) and dropping on to the boards of the landing with hardly enough strength in his hands to break apart his hardtack dinner, teeth not what they had been. Staring at the biscuits as if under a hypnotic weariness for he didn't know how long, then shaking himself out of it and eating and after a time looking outward again, at first at nothing then at the dams and canals again, and at the house off on a rise among the handful of mulberry trees where the man with the black hat was standing at the porch railing watching his flats squeeze through the gates and into the river—a woman appearing beside him who might as well have been Julia herself as whoever she was for the effect of lifting Daws away to the old man on the porch at Honey Hill and the 'daughter' and 'Take his boxes, Loders.'

When he looked again the man was alone at the rail and two men in uniform were halting their horses in the yard, speaking a few words to the man on the porch then dismounting, one

The Affair at Honey Hill

of them climbing the steps, pulling himself up with a hand on the banister, the other taking both bridles and leading the horses off as if discreetly out of earshot—all of it as meaningless to Daws as fine print without his glasses.

And as remote from his living worries as paper characters in a book: early dark and turning cold and a wind rising, and he and Sibley on one of the flats, floating it down on the yellow-orange current between the yellow-orange marshes, poles to sheer them off the sawgrass banks, off other flats, off the granite piles of the bridge when they got there, a sweep at the stern that he thought offered about as much control over their course as a man's intentions over his own (in Daws's history not much, he would have said today).—Sibley still talking about Pike: 'I figure the reason Pike and the General got along so good was Pike wanted to do something bold that would make him a hero, and there was the General planning this bold march to make himself a hero too.'

'You better keep your eyes on the river.'

'And he wanted to be a hero because he didn't like being named for a' Indian,' pushing with his pole and changing the course of the flat enough to save them from smashing against the center pier of the bridge as they swept past like an arrow, the current helping too, swinging them away from the stone triangle pointed up-

67

stream like a ship's prow and foaming with what his father at the shore used to call 'a bone in her teeth,' the triangle rising three or four feet above the water and flat on top, the pier itself rising behind it, rusty iron rungs of a sort of emergency ladder set into the mortar and stepping up the granite blocks to the girders and the tracks. The daylight too weak for him and his eyes to tell if something was hanging beside the rungs (a cord? a piece of string?) and so quickly past it on the squeezed-in swiftness it was only afterward in the river below that he realized he had seen it; but more than that, had seen something moving on the cord. That might have been a frayed fiber in the wind. Or a bird's gray feather caught on the cord. Or a twist of paper from one of the sentries above. He remembered it as a dreamy wisp of smoke. 'Did you see a cord back there? A sort of string?'

'Cord? String?'

'Hanging by the pier, the other side.'

Not worth answering but turning to look back, both of them, as if such a cord would still be visible from the distance they had drifted, and on the upstream side of the pier anyway (and on the dream side for its half-reality), and seeing the lightning-quick stab of the explosion, so quick you felt that it struck, recoiled and struck again before you heard it,—then heard it

The Affair at Honey Hill

with the rolling shock to your senses of a close-by cannon firing over your head, hurled backward on the gust of sound, reverberations settling then or seeming to change into a quiet that denied everything, then into hardly human vocal cords in hardly human stress, into plunging timbers in the water, plunging bodies, one long-haired boy surfacing with his mouth wide open, no breath to scream with, upriver, beyond help from them, no flame at first but as the current carried them on, fires starting in the tarred planks and crossties.

The spreading quiet of a railroad station after the train whips by, and the two of them speechless in the emptiness (speechless except for Sibley's one-time 'Didn't I tell you!'), drifting on, trying to use the sweep and the pole to turn them back and only able to swing a little way out of the current and giving it up, and hearing a whistle out of the sawgrass that might have been meant to pass for a marsh bird but was different enough to get their attention and seeing a figure up to his bare waist in the river as if to wash the sawgrass lacerations on his chest, waving at them one-armed signals of some sort that suggested to Daws it might be a wounded sentry flung off the bridge, then wading in deeper and swimming toward them with one arm, pushing like a frog, dragging the other arm as if unwilling to abandon an injured comrade, Daws pulling on the sweep to throw the flat nearer or try to, Sibley leaning from the bow.

And in a minute shouting some old-man's out-of-date profanity and 'Pike! That's the son of a bitch! That's Wicklow! That's Pike!' jabbing at the man's head and one shoulder. 'Where's my gun? They kept my gun!' And the man grabbing the pole but not able to hold on to it with one hand and going under. Daws trying to steer away with the sweep and feeling a sudden weight on the end that could only be the man (Pike or Wicklow or whatever Yank) and dipping the sweep and twisting it until there was a plunging sound and the sweep was free again, a spurt of exaltation through his chest at avenging the burned and wounded and dead and drowned, fires on the bridge now and ropes being thrown from the bank, some at movements in the water that might have been survivors or rescuers of survivors, some at upriver flats to pull them ashore, the exultation fading out before a spreading uneasiness at being the one to have avenged them. Telling himself as they drifted on that he hadn't really taken this man's life but only turned aside from saving him, looked the other way; the man might have saved himself, might be enough of a swimmer to have reached the marsh again, might have survived, (at any rate survived for someone else's vengeance more ironhearted than Daws's)—as

The Affair at Honey Hill

if trying to talk himself out of an accusation, escape the pain of being wounded, throw off an infection, the war-disease. Forget it! The man had taken other men's lives, was an eager player in this mad checker game swapping life for life —and yet a log behind them half submerged in the river became for him the man swimming or floating after them, following him like the black crag following Wordsworth's boy in the stolen boat.

And following him through two days of winter rain (though at more and more of a distance) then two of colder weather to the City Docks and the GRAYS ripping up the planks to make flooring for the pontoons and the flats; then a strong wind setting from the northwest as the sun went down, blowing in the smoke-smells of burning Georgia, gunsmoke, pine-smoke, a tarred smoke floating down ten miles from the smoldering bridge, blowing the fog away but also blowing the rice straw off the planks as fast as they could scatter it to deaden the wheel sounds, whipping up waves on the river large enough to rock the pontoons (the flats, here on the main channel, and end-to-end for being too few), twist the planks as if wringing out what was left of the rainwater, the whole bridge making a jogglingboard closer to the water than the one to the *Leesburg* under Sibley and Wicklow-Pike, all of it steadying a little under the weight of the fieldpieces and the gun crews pushing them and pulling, the teams waiting behind on the cobblestones to be led across by hand, by overage hands not fit for much else.

And hardly fit for doing that with any competence—in the middle of the river one of the mounts in front of Daws pounding in a nervous flurry at a lurch of the bridge, shouted at, pounding again and breaking the grip of the overage hands and shying off the jogglingboard upstream into the water, Daws's two halters snapping tight in sympathy then relaxing.

'Let him go, let him go! Keep moving! Don't stop!' from somewhere out of the half-dark, authority in the tone, and the parade starting to move again.

And then a harsh countermanding *'Get him!'* and a black soldier dropping over into a flat, fishing in the water and grabbing the wet reins as the horse floundered under the planks, holding him, patting him and talking to him in quiet mumbling stable talk. Then, 'Stay with him, Loders, I'll send a batteau.'

Daws leaving them, leaving his impulse to stay, flushed onward by the thousands at his back—on to a solid road across an island (or solid as churned-up mud could be, not bouncing and twisting, corduroyed, some of it), and then another bridge, and another, shorter now and

The Affair at Honey Hill

steady on backwater creeks and inlets, stumbling on as if divided in half, one part of him thirty miles on to Ferebeeville and Honey Hill as if circling round a center of his life, the other back on the jogglingboard bridge with Loders and the man he knew so well and whose voice he had now heard for the first time.

Or thought he knew so well, knowing the mold that had shaped him, the wife that had.— Loders setting him straight (without intending to) on the starboard deck of the *Winona* with the other prisoners (none of them shackled— who would want to escape to more battles?), the *Wissachickon* up the Tulifinny astern, two cables' lengths a voice said as if it mattered, the *Harvest Moon* ahead, and the rest downstream out of sight toward the Sound, tugs, barges, everything, withdrawing at last—'Mission accomplished'? 'Mission abandoned'?, depending on where you were looking from—slowed by the incoming tide as if on purpose to show him Cheeves Bluff and the half-burned sticks of his fire and the gone-to-rack hut and Julia on the quilt with her knees pushed out, all stirring in his mind ready to escape even if the prisoners weren't, overhead on the superstructure the rocker-arm a heart (young) pumping, never missing a beat: 'Colonel worried about Miss Julia. Didn't know where she was, how she was, nothing.'

'I understood they were divorced.'

'Something like that but he worried just the same, specially after he saw Mr. John. Wrote her lots of times but she didn't answer. "Didn't get the letter," he'd say, and write her again. Asked about her when he wrote the Reverend but the old man never mentioned Madam, talked about the young men, Mr. Boyd and Mr. John, about the church book he was writing, about it looked like everything but Miss Julia. Colonel wrote one of the gentlemen in business with him, could he find something about her for him? was she all right? was she married? living in Savannah? anything, but nothing came of it. The officers in one of the companies had a colored cook who could read and write and I paid him to write Rosanna for me, she might know something. Never a word. Gilbert could have written for her, but never heard a word. And it seemed like the more he tried to find out about her the more he worried when he couldn't. Made him mean sometimes.

'Treated me like a brother, good to me but rough too, rough with the smooth like a brother. Bought me clothes at the Quartermaster's, corporal's uniform, paid me a corporal's pay, said if anybody said anything to say I was his orderly, talk to him, say I answered to him, only him. It was all right, nobody bothered me. Worries plentiful enough to go round without borrowing somebody else's. Didn't have much extra talk. Friendly with his officers but not much socializing. "Do this, do that." He'd call them together, "What do you think, Lieutenant? I'm listening, Captain? Major?" up the ranks from the youngest. Then hand out flat on the table or box or whatever was in front of him and, "Here's what we do," or "Let me sleep on it, I'll know tomorrow." Toe-the-mark Ferebee they called him behind his back, Old Toe-the-mark. Not very popular I'd guess. But fair. A good soldier. They trusted him.

'But he'd talk to me by the hour, by the mile, riding along. There's lots of space between fights in a war, lots of miles and waiting around, and he talked about home to me, about the Low-Country, the Old Place, the Reverend, Old Miss his mamma, mostly about Young Miss. Of course his Old Place was different from mine, but they sometimes overlapped or almost did. We meant the same thing when we said home, the crabs and shrimp, the wind full of salt, the Reverend in the pulpit singing louder than anybody else, a black hole in his beard from singing loud—all that. I remember one day up there, it was quiet, must have been a Sunday because it was General Burnside over there and he wouldn't fight on Sunday. A band was playing over on their side and it up and played *Dixie* and all of us yelled, then it played *Yankee*

The Affair at Honey Hill

Doodle and they all yelled, and then it played *Home Sweet Home* and everybody yelled. He was listening and he laughed a little and said, "Crazy war!" Said, "You need two languages to have a war," thinking of Mexico I reckon.

'Sometimes his leg bothered him, the old wound he got down there. Cramps in it. Pained him a lot sometimes. Showed me how to make him up a hot-mud poultice and lay it on. Seemed to ease him. Didn't complain much. I told him once he ought to complain more and he said he knew of a soldier rode horseback all the way from France to Russia suffering from piles and didn't complain.—Picked him a hatful of blackberries one night to go with his supper. It was up there around Sharpsburg, September I think. He ate them in his fingers one at a time, looking off, then said he and Miss Julia had gone off berry-picking the odd time soon after they were married and he brought her to Honey Hill. Left her there when the *Oglethorpes* went to Texas.'

Daws mumbling, 'Yes, I know,' and Loders nodding, 'Yes sir, you know. You came to help the Reverend along about then.'

And going on after a minute, the guard walking by in his good watertight shoes, 'Sometimes it looked to me like he didn't care what happened to him. I remember once two battle lines facing each other, waiting and watching. Part of them you could see, part you couldn't on account of some trees. He wanted to know what was over there, how strong they were. You could get a pretty good idea by counting their flags but the trees hid some of the flags, or might have hid some. He stood there a minute like he might send somebody crawling over in the woods to count the flags, then without saying anything to anybody, me or anybody else, he got on his horse and rode straight over toward the line. Nobody fired at him, they didn't understand, must have thought he was a messenger or something. When he got close he wheeled and spurred down the line as fast as he could gallop. And those people over there started cheering, not firing a shot, just cheering the whole way. The General was fit to be tied. Called him in. "Something like that again, sir, and I'll put you in chains!" "Yes sir." "Mission for a scout." "Yes sir. I saw signs of cavalry over there, sir." "Mhm. You did? Sit down a minute."

'But Colonel'd keep coming back to Madam, no mention of her for a while, maybe a week or two, then Young Miss again. He said to me, someplace up there I don't remember, riding along before the column, the band back there striking up now and then, he said, "Miss Julia was married before, you know." I said, "No sir, I didn't know that." "Well, engaged to be married. Ring and all that. A young doctor in Savannah. Had been a roomer at their house in

Broughton Street, her mother rented out the top floors." '

Daws said, 'Drayton Street,' and Loders said, 'He said Broughton. Said he didn't mind there'd been somebody else, he loved her. And said he didn't think anything when the baby, Mr. Boyd, seemed to come early. Said, "I say seemed because we had been together in Savannah—you know how it is." "Yes sir." "It was years later that I began to wonder. Really not until John was born. I lost my temper then. Kept thinking about a damn-fool enlisted man came to my tent out in Texas. Would I speak to the Sergeant? Why? What's the trouble? The man's wife cooked for the officers mess, the Sergeant was always hanging round her, would I speak to him? I said, 'Haven't you got a gun? Can't you defend your own family? Get out!' And it wasn't five minutes before there was a shot in the cook tent. The Sergeant was dead. I thought of doing what the soldier did. You've got a gun, Ferebee. Can't you defend your own family! I did nothing. Except behave badly, treat her badly. There was no more love for her left in me, or ever would be, I would have sworn to that."

' "But, Loders," (after a while, calling my name but really talking more to himself than me—he did that some days). I said, "Yes sir," when he didn't go on, (it was better for him

The Affair at Honey Hill

if he went on talking), and he said with a sort of smile in the way he said it more than in any change in his face, "You remember the prickly pears there by the side steps, trying to get rid of the prickly pears. It's no use chopping them off at the ground, that spreads them. And if you dig them up you have to get every little root or they'll come back. And if you overlook a piece of the tops on the ground, first good rain and it will begin to take root." Said his love grew back like he had missed a piece of the root in the soil. Returned to it another day as if he'd been thinking, said Madam's love was a little different, was more like a new plant taking root from a piece of the top left on the ground. Said it didn't need much watering to grow on, and didn't much care who watered it.

'Not just him but everybody talking about their womenfolks at home, thinking about them, writing them, looking to the day they could get a pass or a furlough (or a piece of shrapnel, not too bad) and go home for a while. Once he got hit in the side by a spent grape shot but it wasn't serious enough. Knocked him down and stunned him and lodged in his coat. He put it in his pocket, "for good luck," he said. No home for Colonel to go home to anyhow, the old house locked up, windows boarded up, abandoned (Mr. Gilbert kept an eye on it, Reverend gave him a few acres not far off—wrote me once), the old man in Columbia with Dr. Boyd and his family, Mr. John in the army somewhere he didn't know where; talked about them all, worried about them, the war seeming to be blowing their way—Chickamauga, Chattanooga, then into Georgia—worried about them all but mostly about Madam, maybe because for a year or two he had no news at all.

'We got a big surprise once, must have been the summer of '64, sometime after Petersburg and hot. I had a fire going, was fixing to start Colonel's supper, he had just got back, was taking a nap. A young man came up to me, a corporal, asked where he could find Colonel Ferebee, then looked at me hard and said Wasn't I Loders? It was Mr. John, and I shook Colonel's shoulder and said, "You've got a visitor." And Mr. John, there by the cot, saluted his daddy, heels together and all that, Colonel blinking his eyes and standing up, laughing and patting his arm like saluting didn't matter but I think he was pleased at the soldierness behind it. Almost the first thing he asked was, "What do you hear from your mother?" Mr. John, Corporal John, said Not much. Said he had a letter some time back from a girl in Savannah who had seen her at a meeting of the Georgia Ladies Gunboat Fund, there with a tall man who had contributed $1,000, looking well, didn't get a chance to speak to her. He said his mother mentioned the meeting in a letter but—laughing a little—didn't mention her escort or the thousand dollars: "Mother plays 'em close to the chest, you know," and Colonel said Yes, he knew.

'He left next day, had to get back, but his visit seemed to make Colonel think about home more than ever. When he heard from Dr. Boyd that Sherman was in central Georgia—" 'making Georgia howl,' they say he says, seems to be heading for the Low-Country" (a margin note in Reverend's pencil said, "My History not ended but looks like the House of God is")— Colonel applied for transfer to the Southeast Department and for a short leave to go do what he could for them; anxious about his father in Columbia (the application read), about his wife last heard from in the path of the invading army. The General initialed it and sent it up and before long Colonel paraded the Regiment, band and everything, and turned it over and I packed up and we set out for the railroad.

'Dr. Boyd brought the Reverend down to the depot to see him between trains, mighty feeble but his mind all right, said it was nip and tuck which got to the end first and everybody thought he meant himself or the war but he meant himself or his History of the House of God. "Couldn't bring it all with me, Olivious. If you have a chance I wish you would get the rest out of my desk drawers in the study and send it to me." "Yes sir, I will." "Gilbert has a key if you've misplaced yours." No mention of Miss Julia and when Colonel asked, the Doctor shook his head and talked away from it. The Reverend handed me some money as we got in the cars, mumbled, "Here, Loders, put this in your pocket" like he was asking me a favor.— The train people said I couldn't ride with Colonel. He said, "I'm a Confederate soldier, this man is my orderly, don't bother me!" And that settled it. You didn't argue with Colonel when he spoke like that, eyebrows down.'

The Ladies Gunboat Fund no longer in existence—the gunboat built, launched and maybe on the bottom of the Savannah River by that time—but some of the ladies still to be found and 'the first lady Colonel talked to had a clear memory of a large donation to the Fund by the owner of Silk Hope Plantation, Mr. Robert Fillious.'

Daws said, 'And you rode up to Silk Hope and talked to Mr. Fillious on his porch, I know.'

'Yes sir.'

'And Miss Julia was just inside the house.'

'I don't know about that. I just know he didn't invite Colonel except to the porch, just said no he had met Miss Julia, charming lady, but could be no help to Colonel in finding her. Said he saw Madam at the meeting but that was a long time ago, went on talking about the war,

The Affair at Honey Hill

about his flats floating off down the river. It was the night the bridge went up.'

'Yes, I know.'

'They built the pontoon bridge with the flats,' stopping as if there weren't any more to tell, the guard walking down the deck and back with his gun in his left elbow like a fifteenth-century Madonna and Child, the paddles slushing. Then, 'When the horse went off the planks into the river I grabbed his bridle from the bow of a flat and held him while Colonel went to find a batteau, the current pulling the horse out downstream, or the tide, or both, horse swimming, nervous, excited. No batteau to be found over there in the dark, half-dark, but one of the engineer people turned up a rope, came back with Colonel on foot, no good trying to ride back with everything going the other way and the planks hardly wide enough for the wagons. I could see Colonel's leg was bothering him, saber hanging, getting in his way, the engineer soldier impatient behind him with Colonel not moving fast enough. They threw me an end of the rope and I tied a good slipknot in the bridle. Idea was to let the rope out to where the horse could swim below the flats and lead him over to the far bank.'

Stopping again as the guard strolled by though it was nothing the guard cared about, or anybody else, Daws thought, but himself and Lo-

The Affair at Honey Hill

ders, stopping really, he wondered later, because he didn't want to live it again. Then going on, 'I don't know what happened. Maybe he couldn't move quick enough on his leg, tripped on the rope as it snapped up tight, the horse swinging away. Maybe he just lost his footing on the planks, slippery anyhow from the rice straw. Maybe his leg got a cramp. Maybe he just didn't care any more what happened to him. Anyway, he went under between two of the flats, saber, sidearms and everything, came up twenty feet downstream, or seemed to, you couldn't see much, not calling out or anything, might have been a piece of driftwood I saw. I was out of my coat, half over the side of the flat when some officer on the planks shouted at me to stay where I was and I stopped till I remembered he said I answered to him and nobody else and I went on over. But wasn't any use. He was way down the current by then, must have been, though you couldn't see him. Somebody paddled out in a batteau with a lantern, pulled me over the end.'

Silent again, then seeming to reappear at a distance like a diver too, giving his head a sort of snapping shake as if to get water out of his ears—get the memory out of his mind—and leaping to, 'Saw you with your canteen, followed you to the spring, reckoned you'd want to know about Colonel.'

The Affair at Honey Hill

Waiting a dozen turns of the paddles while his decision was taking shape to let that end it for Loders, the rest of no concern to anyone but him and Julia, wishing it might be the end of it for himself too instead of turning round and round in his thoughts like the paddles, patrolling back and forth in front of him holding him prisoner like the guard. But, one question: 'Did Colonel ever find Miss Julia?'

'Not exactly find her, no sir. But Madam was in the house, so he said. Said he could tell by the perfume she wore.'—The words tossing into Daws's mind an association so incongruous as to be laughable if it had been a day for laughing,

A strange invisible perfume hits the sense
Of the adjacent wharfs . . .
Upon her landing, Anthony sent to her———

The GRAYS all over the city 'wharfs' prying up the boards to make flooring for the pontoons and the flats, a plan somewhere (he hoped), in somebody's mind if not yet on paper, a pencil sketch of how the end would be, a study of a hand or foot for future use. From the wharf's edge a makeshift gangway of planks laid across the bare black net of piling to the street, crowded then with refugees from the deck of the *Let Her Be* picking their way to shore, most of them white, and one, as Daws straightened shoulders to steal a look, the man on the dock at Silk Hope (Fillious?) and reaching back a gloved hand for the gloved hand of a lady to guide her over the loose planks, a lady with a short veil close against her face tied at the back of her neck who was to him as clearly Julia as the one in the carriage at the parade of the JASPER GREENS, and Julia reaching back to the black hand of a young woman loaded down with parcels one of which was a covered birdcage, none of them giving a thought to the dirty soldiers balanced on crowbars and mallets on the barnacled piling.

Waiting for the sergeant to turn his head and escaping in time to see them from a distance as they gave up trying to hire a conveyance and walked away (no hacks today, as if erased by the constant rubbing sound of cannonfire louder than yesterday). Following them over empty sidewalks until they entered the arcade before the Planters' Hotel and in a moment disappeared, he stopping against a fluted iron post in sudden indecision. What now? What did he hope for? could he hope for?—and a flock of questions he should have asked himself before. A hurried word or two with her? Certainly not with her and her 'gentleman-friend', and what possible way was there to separate them? His eyes turning involuntarily toward the river and the wharf as if all but ready to come to his

The Affair at Honey Hill

senses and go back, then facing the hotel again in time to see Fillious stride hurriedly through the door and cross the street diagonally in the direction of City Hall, continuing to watch as he shook hands with two men on the steps and entered with them as if for a common purpose.

Glancing then at his dingy uniform, almost as if searching for a substitute reason to abandon his errand, and catching sight of a show window of men's furnishings that seemed to remove for him the last of his restraints. Buying a gray shirt in the shop (the only customer and the one clerk nervously blinking at each far-off cannon and window-rattle), an officer's shirt but most of it would be hidden if he buttoned his jacket, brushed at the spots and stains and buttoned it. The clerk shaking his head when asked if he knew of a barber's shop open today, then saying he might try Mr. Balzeau round the corner, Mr. Balzeau lived upstairs and might accommodate him.

Which *J. Balzeau, Wig Maker & Hair-Dresser* was considerate enough to do. 'No hot water today, Captain,' at Daws's moving toward a door marked BATHS.

But Daws washing head to foot anyway with Mr. Balzeau's worn cake of disinfectant soap, hardly noticing the temperature of the water for the string of questions moving through his head like the close-coupled cars of a supply train (when there had been such things): Fillious, or whoever he was, would he have come back by now? Would the hotel clerk insist on sending a boy with him to knock on her door? Could he pursuade the clerk to let him go up alone? Would her maid be with her? How would she feel at seeing him again? Would she send the maid away? Would she even allow him to come in? Would it be better to send up a note first? Would this? would that?—and he was sitting under a flowered sheet for a trimming of his hair and beard (glancing away from the gray snips falling among the flowers). 'A dash of bay rum, Captain?' 'Not today, Mr. Balzeau,' even if there should be for her a whiff of Mr. Balzeau's soap. And the enveloping question that could still be revived to take care of everything—give it all up and retreat to the wharf?

Most of the questions vanishing as he entered the hotel lobby, the square partly-carpeted space as empty as the streets, the side of a man's busy head beyond a grille marked CASHIER, small white columns not unlike the memorable ones in the church, two fireplaces across from each other, one of them dark, closed off with a blower, the other burning a sleepy coal fire with Julia beside it in a wicker chair, bare head tilted up as she talked to a man with a pad and pencil in his black hands. A tulip glass of wine that looked like Madeira flickered in the firelight on a knee-high table.

'Six oysters, Hunter, do you think? Or would you suggest a dozen?'

'As you say, Madam.'

'Hungry soldiers, you know. They've just walked three hundred miles—or their horses have. Nevertheless, six.'

'Very good, Madam,' writing on the pad.

'And a chilled Moselle, not too cold, can you do that, Hunter?'

'Oh yes, Madam.'

'And after the oysters, baked shad perhaps? —No, not shad. All those bones. They'd say we tried to choke them.'

'Pompano, Madam? It's the season.'

'I'll think, Hunter, and talk to you tomorrow. It won't be until the day after anyway, and maybe the next. Prepare for twenty, no, twenty-five.'

'Yes, Madam,' filling the half-empty tulip glass and moving away over the green-and-white checkerboard tiles, Julia jotting down something on a paper she returned to a lace bag, stuffing it in in a careless ball as redolent of times past as the perfume, the sort of offhandedness with which she had put aside the mystery dinner for twenty-five hungry soldiers whose horses had walked three hundred miles.

Listening to all of it from a few yards off, more for the sound of her voice than what it said, disappointed to find her preoccupied with thoughts so distant from the area of his own but having come too far to change his mind now. Yet changing his half-formed intention of simply walking up in front of her and saying, 'Julia?' in a question as if not quite sure. Changing it to a careless three or four steps toward the fire, pretending to warm his hardly presentable hands and falling back on the weather.

'Turning colder, Madam, I'd say,' to the fire, wondering suddenly (too late) if she would know his voice, and since she didn't seem to, wondering when it would begin to stir her memory. Then wondering most of all about his next words. Indeed—with her silence—whether there would be any, whether Madam too was turning colder.

Which seemed a possibility as she appeared quietly to appraise him then slowly took a sip from the glass and set it down. Then she looked at him with a trace of a smile and said, Yes, she believed it was. Silence for a time except for a now-and-then almost sleepy cannon-rattle in a window, then, Would Madam object if he sat down for a minute?

'Please do,' with a nod at a chair like her own, her nod going on to become a sort of hostess glance at the partly closed diningroom doors and a signal to a waiter for another glass. 'You are with the garrison in the city?' in a tone of putting the rough soldier at his ease with a topic he was equipped to talk about, and he saying, 'Unfortunately,' with a smirk, wishing to demonstrate with a sort of performing word that he was something more than rough soldier, the waiter transferring a second tulip glass from his tray to the table and filling both.

'Not so "unfortunately," perhaps,' the waiter clicking away over the tiles. 'I've heard you may be allowed to escape.'

'Oh, do you think so?'

'Rebel cotton, that's what they want, not Rebel prisoners.'

He said he hoped so, and she raised her glass as if for Happy Birthday! and, friendliness itself, said, 'Let us hope,' he raising his with, 'Yes, let's hope.'

'I have a gentleman friend who knows everything. He says if Savannah is surrendered by midnight tomorrow they won't destroy the city. He is with the Mayor now, the Mayor and Aldermen, they'll be having supper. He says it may take half the night to persuade them but Atlanta makes a good argument. They would have to go out under a flag of truce and surrender the city, not the Army but the city. He says they won't like that.' (She didn't know him! Not yet, anyway. The beard and the gray in it, the years between the dim church and now, all the other faces in her memory since then hiding him. All he needed to do was say, 'Julia,' yet saying it seemed an intrusion on her comfortable unawareness of him, an asking for something whose value lay mostly in its being offered —and not saying it might show him Julias he didn't know, today's). 'My friend says natives should always throw flowers to the conquering army, and usually do,' smiling a surprising Julia smile.

Thinking a minute then saying with a smile of his own, 'So you are planning a shower of oysters and pompano,' she looking at him hard for an instant as if about to see him, then briefly laughing at comic soldier and serious again.

'Mr. Green is giving it, asked me to help. The General wants to make a speech, wants to read the telegraphic dispatch he is sending the President. It has circulated, my friend has seen it, says it's really aimed at the front page of the *New York Herald,* something like, "Sir. I beg to present you as a Christmas gift the City of Savannah, with thirteen million dollars in bales of cotton." The General says Mr. Lincoln peculiarly enjoys such pleasantries.—But excuse me! Who cares about all that? What about *you?* Tell me about yourself. Have you been in the army long?'

'Decades, I'd say,' edgy, wanting to exist for her, tempted to forget his reasons for not saying 'Julia,' she silent, almost as if waiting for him

The Affair at Honey Hill

to continue, turning the glass by the stem. Then, as though deciding, not looking at him, quietly to her slender hands, 'I'm having supper served in my rooms, would you care to join me?'—to a stranger, a strange soldier, a strange not-too-clean soldier! The shock of it seeming to resolve his uncertainty, throwing it into the first words that came to mind: 'I don't believe you know me, Julia.'

'Know you? Should I? What do you mean?' staring at him as if letting half-formed questions become half-formed answers, then fully-formed, and setting down the glass so vehemently it fell and shattered on the tiles, and running to the stairs and up them with a flash of white stockings—the Julia of the ambrotype mounting the steps of the train for Silk Hope, and the Julia on the steps by the spring. But most of all, the Julia fleeing the pushing-together of so many years, so many Julias, so many betrayals—so many indelibles.

Follow her?—As well try crossing the broken spans of the bridge—

'Hit the deck, you lousy Rebs! Fall in!' in much the same bellow as the 'Put-up-your-hands!' at the Flowing Well, and they were marched off through the gateway of what had been Fort Beauregard, 'FORT BURNSIDE' now in exultant fresh paint over the portcullis—for the General who wouldn't fight on Sunday.

93